DEPTHS AWAKENED

LAKE LAVENDER SERIES

USA TODAY BESTSELLING AUTHOR
PERSEPHONE AUTUMN

BETWEEN WORDS PUBLISHING LLC

DEPTHS AWAKENED

LAKE LAVENDER SERIES

USA TODAY BESTSELLING AUTHOR
PERSEPHONE AUTUMN

BETWEEN WORDS PUBLISHING LLC

Depths Awakened

Copyright © 2019 by Persephone Autumn

www.persephoneautumn.com

ISBN: 978-1-951477-00-4 (Ebook)

ISBN: 978-1-951477-62-2 (Paperback)

Editor: Elizabeth Nover | Razor Sharp Editing

Editor: Ellie McLove | My Brother's Editor

Proofreader: Gemma Woolley | Gem's Precise Proofreads

Cover Design: Abigail Davies | Pink Elephant Designs

BOOKS BY PERSEPHONE AUTUMN

Artist Duet

Blank Canvas

Abstract Passion

Novellas

Reese

Penny

Stone Bay Series

Broken Sky—Prequel

Standalone Romance Novels

Sweet Tooth

Transcendental

Poetry Collections

Ink Veins

Broken Metronome

Slipping From Existence

PUBLISHED UNDER P. AUTUMN

Standalone Non-Romance Novels

By Dawn

For my twin flame, the one who makes me whole,
believes in me always, is my strength when
I need it, and makes me better every day.
I love you with every fascicle of my being!
Forever and ever, always!

PROLOGUE
GEOFFREY

"I'm not ready for you to go," I whisper against our hands. Her hand rests cold and limp in mine, her body unmoving. Charlotte hasn't responded to my touch since yesterday afternoon. "I don't think I can say goodbye."

Not a word. Just the harsh sounds of her lungs begging for air.

I thought we'd have our whole lives together. Turns out fate had other plans.

All I want is another five minutes. That isn't asking for too much, is it? To hear her voice one last time. Catch one final glimpse of her sparkling green irises. Tell her *I love you* and that I will never forget her.

I could never forget her.

The fluorescent light above her bed hums, the only light illuminating the room flickering as often as my heart skips. I take a deep breath, close my eyes, and concentrate on matching my rhythm to the one on Charlotte's monitor.

Tha-thump. Tha-thump. Tha-thump.

Over the last week, I have memorized the rhythm of her heart. Although the sound is mechanical, hearing that constant beat has kept me alive as well. I lay my head beside our hands, my eyes heavy. I haven't slept in days, wanting to be alert if Charlotte wakes.

Just as I'm drifting off, a blaring alarm fills the room. On the monitor, her vitals scream and my heart stops. I forget how to breathe.

A flat, red line scrolls across the screen, a red zero flashing beside it.

No. Please don't let this be happening. "I need help in here!"

Within seconds, nurses and doctors flood the room. A bulky machine is wheeled in behind them. A chill spreads from head to toe and I freeze next to Charlotte.

"Sweetie, you need to step aside. Let the doctors help her." But it takes me too long to absorb the command before the kindly nurse is shoving me out of the way.

The calm quiet from ten minutes ago is gone. Organized chaos takes its place.

The oxygen tube is yanked from Charlotte's nose and replaced with a silicone mask attached to an air pump in the nurse's hand. She squeezes the bulbous bag, forcing oxygen into her lungs.

Each time Charlotte's chest rises and falls, my heart beats more sluggishly, my palms damp and clammy. The monitor continues screaming in the background, one of the doctors watching the flat line while performing chest compressions, asking one of the nurses to silence the alarm.

After a minute, the doctor removes her hands and my chest hollows out. *Has she given up? So soon?*

My questions are answered when a nurse takes a pair of surgical scissors to the front of Charlotte's gown, cutting the flimsy material down her midline and exposing her torso. As soon as the frigid hospital air hits her bare chest, the doctor slaps two large adhesive pads into place. Gooseflesh prickles my limbs and my body convulses.

In the few seconds needed to charge the defibrillator, I age eighty years.

"Clear!" the doctor bellows.

Every person aiding in her care raises their hands, taking a half step from the bed. The doctor presses a button, and I suck in a breath as Charlotte's body jolts upward from the sterile sheets of the hospital bed. Every pair of eyes is glued to the monitor, mine included, waiting for a response.

If there is a god in the universe, please don't let this happen to Charlotte. I beg you.

The flat line on the monitor is unchanged. I pinch my eyes tight and repeat my previous prayer.

"Charging..." a nurse says, her calm demeanor shredding my sanity.

The nurse with the air resuscitation bag returns the silicone triangle to Charlotte's face, pumping the bag to a rhythm in her head, a steady flow of oxygen pouring into Charlotte's incapable lungs. I shuffle to my left, stepping out of the path of the hospital staff to get a better vantage point of Charlotte's pale body.

"Clear!"

Charlotte's body bows off the bed again, and her hollowness resonates in my chest. The voltage does nothing to restart her heart, the muted heart monitor remains unchanged. The nurse at the head of the bed forces more oxygen into her chest before the defibrillator fully recharges for another round.

"Clear!"

Everyone steps back, the image of the room blurring

behind the haze of tears filling my eyes. *Come on, Charlotte. Fight! For you. For us. Fight!*

The pounding of footsteps and tear-filled screams enter the room, Charlotte's mother running to my side. Sobs wrack her frame as she squeezes my hand tight. I want to console her, but then who will do that for me?

Another charge from the defibrillator pierces Charlotte's flesh and runs to her heart.

But there's nothing.

After multiple attempts to resuscitate her, the team pauses, exchanging glances, an unspoken agreement passing through the room. Removing the adhesive pads from her chest and setting them on the cart, a doctor closes the front of Charlotte's gown, looks up at the clock over the doorframe and calls out the official time of death.

Charlotte's mom falls to the floor beside me, clutching her stomach and dropping her head to the sterile, bleach-scented linoleum. Her loud cries echo out of the room and fill the entire floor of the hospital.

My feet have turned to stone—heavy and incapable of moving. My chest is a forest fire, the burn spreading from my heart into my lungs. My vision fogs, the room disappearing.

My world has stopped moving. Life transitions from living to existing.

Because I don't want this life if she isn't a part of it. It will always be her. Only her.

As my vision clears, my mind slips into a newfound numbness. One that feels as silent and permanent as the heart monitor's flat red line.

CHAPTER 1
MAGDALENA

"What are you doing here, Mags?" Lessa shrieks, coming around the corner and yanking me into a tight hug.

"I thought I'd be adventurous this morning. Plus, I love seeing you," I manage to say as she wrings my torso like a wet cloth. Her hugs are the best. But sometimes she can hug the life right out of a person.

When she realizes I'm having trouble breathing, Lessa steps back and releases me from her grip. "Sorry. It's just so nice to see you outside of dinners at your house. Did you want to order something?"

She steps back behind the counter and stands opposite me, poised and ready to take my order.

"Yes, please. Can I have a hot green tea and a blueberry bagel, whipped and excited," I laugh as I place the order, my cheeks heating.

Lessa is the proud owner of Java and Teas Me, an eclectic coffee and tea café in our small town of Lake Lavender—named for the lavender fields near the to 's only waterfront

—a hidden gem less than an hour from Olympia. When she proposed the idea of opening the shop to me and Lena, the other part of our trifecta, I almost spit my drink across her business plan.

All of the food on the menu at Java and Teas Me has an eccentric name. The bagel I just ordered... "whipped and excited" means with whipped cream cheese and a dash of cinnamon sugar.

Lessa gives me a wicked grin, knowing how reserved I am. "You got it. Do you want it for here or to go?"

"Here, please. I still need a little me time before I start my day."

Her smile is wide and could make any person's day better. It's one of the many things I love about her. One of the things I envy her.

"Cool. Have a seat wherever and I'll bring it out in a sec."

I weave my way through the throng of tables, passing a handful of college students with earbuds in place and eyes fixated to their laptop screens. Selecting a table on the semi-closed patio, I have a perfect view of the morning sunrise and the sidewalks of Main Street.

Summer mornings are my favorite and the most beautiful. The air is crisp with a slight chill as the scent of piney ever-greens float in the breeze and dawn breaks over the mountains and tree lines. The sky is painted in a spectacular array of pinks and oranges, allowing the cyan of the day to make its morning debut.

The sunrise today is a little pinker than yesterday as I relax in the plush padded wicker chair. I take a deep breath and get lost in my own personal wonderland. A moment later, my tea and bagel are delivered.

"If you'll be here for a bit, I'll come back and chat, but business is starting to pick up," Lessa tells me, regret highlighting her features when she eyes the growing line.

"No worries. We'll catch up later. Love you."

"Love you, too, Mags."

I pick up my mug, cradling it between my palms, and blow on the surface of the steamy beverage. As I settle into the chair, my gaze falls over the women and men strolling down the wide sidewalk. Some peering into storefronts, others grabbing a quick bite or drink before heading to work. Laughter, smiles, and joy highlighting each of their days. The sight sparks envy in my chest.

Today I took a leap. It was time to step outside the four walls of my home for something other than groceries or necessities. It was time to start living again. Time to start breathing after years of routine and care-giving.

I tear off a piece of my bagel and pop it in my mouth, giggling to myself. "I'm finally growing up," I whisper to no one. A rush courses through my veins. It's both invigorating and terrifying.

I can do this. My new motto.

Lessa falls into the chair across from me, my hand slapping against my chest as I gasp.

"You scared the shit out of me."

"Sorry," she tells me, blowing her hair out of her eyes.

"It's great out here. I think I may come here more often." For a moment, I contemplate reaching across the table and closing Lessa's dropped jaw. But I give her a moment to digest what I told her. I'm sure it surprised her as much as it did me.

"I'm sorry, did I just hear you say you plan to come here more often?" she asks, her eyes pinching as she cocks her head.

"You heard correct. I must've had an enlightening dream

last night. I think it's time I try to find myself again. Don't you agree?"

The legs of her chair scrape against the brick below as she pushes up and barrels toward me. Within a beat, I am wrapped in Lessa's arms again, happy I inhaled beforehand. I give her to the count of three and then pat her back, a silent signal to release me from her clutches.

Another ten seconds pass. Another ten seconds that I'm deprived of the ability to breathe. I love the bonding moment, but my lips may be turning a little blue.

"Can't breathe."

In an instant, she releases me. "Sorry, sorry, sorry. I'm just so excited about this. Excited for you!"

At least one of us is excited. Me? I'm a bit queasy and am glad I only ordered a bagel. "Thanks, Lessa. I think it's been a long time coming, but the eureka moment only struck today. Will you help me?"

Her lips form the sweetest smile I've ever seen as she takes my hand in hers. "You know I will. Lena and I are here for anything you need. You know that."

Giving her hand a gentle squeeze, I reply, "I know you are. I could not have asked for two better people in my life." I pause a moment, drawing in a breath. "This is going to sound stupid, but... I don't know how to be *different*. How do I act *normal*?"

She takes my hand in both of hers, cradling it with the gentle nature a mother would a child. "Just be yourself. We'll figure the rest out as we go."

"Just be myself. I can do that," I affirm. "I've been putting more time into packing up Dad's stuff. It's sad, but cathartic. And I think it's helping me move on a little more each day."

"You know Lena and I will help you in a heartbeat. Just say the word."

I crumple my napkin into a ball. "Yeah, I know. But I think boxing everything is helping me transition from mourning to living. I'm only keeping a few mementos from him and Mom. The rest is being donated."

A soft glow lights Lessa's face. "Well, keep us in mind."

I nod before she sweeps me into another hug. It has been challenging to sift through my parents' belongings. Every time I pick up a shirt my dad wore, I'd press it to my nose and inhale his woodsy scent. The thought of never smelling it again swelled my throat and pricked my eyes. Mom's perfume faded from her clothes several years ago, but I kept a bottle of the rosy scent for the days when I miss her most.

"Have you considered getting a job? After you take care of everything, of course," Lessa suggests.

Work had crossed my mind. It would be a huge leap in the right direction. "Yeah, but is it weird that I'm not sure where to begin?"

Her eyes widen as if a lightbulb has gone off in her head. "Why don't you put your degree to some use? You worked your butt off to earn it."

That's an idea worth pondering. And, for the first time in years, a rush has my pulse soaring. "Maybe I'll go talk with Beatrice when I leave here. I'm sure she can guide me in the right direction."

"Yay!" Lessa claps before squeezing me close again, this one brief when she notices the line at the counter growing.

Not wanting to monopolize her time, I shoo her away. After she steps behind the counter and resumes business owner mode, I send her a quick message.

MAGDALENA

> Thanks for everything. Have a great day! See you at dinner tomorrow.

After tapping send, I stash my phone in my purse. She'll respond to me later, once business has slowed down. Grabbing my mug and plate, I head over to the bin and place the dishes in the gray tub.

Just be yourself. We'll figure out the rest out as we go.

As I head for my car, Lessa's affirmation repeats in my thoughts.

Just be myself. I can do this.

One Month Later

The parking lot of Black Silk is bustling. I'd never been here any night except Friday, but I'm sure there was never a slow night. Just as I spot a parking space, I notice Lessa and Lena walking inside, glad they wouldn't be waiting long for my arrival.

We'd started coming to Black Silk two weeks ago—as a celebration for my new job—after Lena overheard a customer raving about it. Within thirty minutes, Lena had found every scrap of information on the internet about the place. Our group text thread blew up as she sent screenshot after screenshot of reviews, telling us the pictures looked amazing. After one visit, we loved it so much it's now a weekly occurrence.

Black Silk was an upscale restaurant but also had an adjoining nightclub upstairs. In the time since we'd been dining here, none of us had climbed the stairs to the second floor. Often, I wondered if the nightclub was worthy of our time—you could never hear a sound from the dining area below.

A short time ago, I may have decided to step out into the world a little more, but I know I wouldn't be the one to initiate the ascension of that staircase.

I walk along the small pathway between the lot and the restaurant, a man stands at a set of tall oak doors and opens them as I approach. Black iron connects the doors to the frame, giving them a medieval vibe. I step inside and thank the man as I pass.

Stepping past the hostess station, I weave my way toward my friends.

The restaurant is both eclectic and elegant.

Charcoal black walls are decorated in an array of black-and-white photographs, sketches, and paintings. Along the ceiling, striking oak beams spanned from one end of the restaurant to the other, the wood stained a medium gray.

Classy, antique lighting hung four feet above each table, adding a soft, dim ambiance to each place setting. The oak tables—matching the sturdy beams above—adorned with pale, stone gray tablecloths and a small candlelit, floral centerpiece.

Adding to their namesake, each person's silverware rested on a black, silk-like napkin.

Lessa and Lena spot me before I reach the table, their hands gesturing a wave in my direction. My chest warms at their enthusiasm to see me and I can't stop the smile that pains my cheeks.

Before I'm able to take my seat, Lena's eyes run up and down my body, giving me a once-over. Her visual assessment has me cringing internally, my smile fading as I fight to not wrap my arms tight around the center of my body.

"Hey, girl. You're looking beautiful, as always. Actually, I'd like to amend that statement. You look *hot* tonight."

Lena, my dear, sweet friend, has a keen eye for fashion. Her business depends on it. But I wasn't so sure about her opinion of me right now. *Hot* was never a word I associated with my appearance, even when I was dressed or dolled up.

And I was neither at the current moment.

Heat stains my cheeks, the fever spreading slow over my chest as I sit in my chair.

"I have no clue what you're talking about," I mumble. "I just reached in the closet and grabbed whatever."

She lets out a low huff, a huff I've heard on more than one occasion. "*Seriously*? You have to know how stunning you look right now. Low cut, black top accentuating your perfect bust. White jeans hugging those amazing legs, which I'd kill for, by the way. Finish it off with the black heels." She pauses and shakes her head. "You know how much I envy you, right? And your hair... it always looks perfect." She cocks her head to the side, then says, "Do you have a date later?"

I open my mouth to respond, but nothing comes. Her assessment and inquisition have me taken aback.

First, she knew I never saw myself as she saw me. Second, she knew I didn't date.

Anyone.

Ever.

At least not since my dad's stroke.

Taking compliments has never been a strength. In fact, compliments are a cloak of awkwardness. They make my stomach twist and knot like a pretzel. A sudden obligation overwhelms me and I feel the need to compliment her in return. Something I'm not prepared for, my brain to mouth filter temporarily out of service.

So, I say the first thing that comes to mind.

"Just a date with the two most amazing women I know." My cheeks heat anew as I mutter, "Thanks for thinking I look hot. But you know I beg to differ."

If someone compared shades of red to my cheeks right now, I'd vote mine were similar to strawberries or hand-picked cherries. I couldn't see myself, but I could feel the sweltering heat of embarrassment as it spread across my flesh.

I take a minute to look down at my attire, confused at what makes something so simple look so alluring. *It's a shirt and a pair of jeans, for crying out loud.*

"I don't *think* anything. I know it. Please take a compliment without doubting it, just this once," Lena cajoles, her matter-of-fact tone meant to settle any further negations.

Accepting compliments is a weakness I've had for years, but a part of me I will continue to work on.

The waiter approaches the table, poised and ready to take our orders. Looking to Lessa and Lena, I subliminally ask for one of them to start. Lessa reads me like a book and speaks up.

Once we've all ordered, he turns on his heel and walks off.

As soon as he's gone, I'm prepared for *the lecture*. It's been the same speech every Friday. Without fail.

Lessa works hard at throwing me her best stink eye, all while trying not to laugh. "Still just water, huh? I thought you were going to live a little, weren't you?"

The first question, I expected. It was as ritualistic as my life.

The second question, on the other hand, hits me like a strike to the gut. It knocks the wind out of me and I'm uncertain how I should respond.

They knew why I didn't drink alcohol when we went out. It went without question.

And tonight would be no exception.

Unbeknownst to me, tonight's version of nagging sat heavier on my shoulders. Even though she was teasing me, the words were loaded with something more I couldn't see or grasp. Resonating in a different place in my chest, a piercing ache beneath my sternum.

The sudden urge to defend myself grew strong. "You know why I don't drink. Not since Mom died. The occasional teasing is getting old. Plus, I don't need alcohol to have a good time." For added effect—and to lighten the mood—I stuck my tongue out at both of them.

"Mags, all we want is for you to relax and enjoy the evening," Lena chimes in.

I could sense the pang of guilt she bore and I didn't want either of them to have that burden.

"Yes, I know. And I love you both for always wanting me to enjoy myself. But I promise, hanging out with the two of you is all I need."

Truer words could not have been said.

Lessa and Lena were better than any other remedy I'd received after each of my parents passed away. Our bond was this invisible life force, an impenetrable bubble no one could pierce.

"I hope that's true because we're headed upstairs tonight," Lessa declares, her face lighting up as if she'd won the lottery. "I've been dying to check out the nightclub since we started coming here."

The excitement of what secrets awaited her up the stairwell made her bouncy. It was adorable and infectious and made my stomach flip.

The waiter returns with our drinks and I sip the cool liquid, my nerves calming a smidge.

"So, Mags, it's perfect timing that you wanted to live a little more. I'm excited to check out the club after dinner. I know nothing about the vibe, but I overheard one of my employees say it was amazing." Lessa beams, her excitement tangible.

I don't think I have seen her quite so giddy in a while. The more she speaks, the higher her volume escalates.

It is no secret she and Lena tried to get me out of the house more often. Always attempting to break me out of my home-body status. And they both agreed my shifts at Statice didn't count toward *getting out there.*

I may have stated I wanted to expand my horizons, but there's nothing wrong with enjoying my own company. As the old saying goes... If it ain't broke, don't fix it.

All I needed was a little tweak.

"What did your employee say?" I ask, my curiosity piqued.

"She wasn't forthcoming with the details. She said everyone should experience it without bias, and to go in open-minded," she explains before adding, "I think it sounds myste-rious and exciting. Am I right?"

I force an uneasy smile, not wanting to put a damper on her good mood. In Lessa's eyes, dinner couldn't finish fast enough. She bounced in her chair like a child begging for the coolest new toy.

Me, on the other hand... I continue to wipe my sweaty palms over my thighs, praying dinner will take hours.

Why would her employee be evasive? It's a nightclub, not the plotline to a movie.

"Doesn't it seem strange they didn't tell you anything about the place?" I question, my voice cracking a little.

Lessa glances at me, and for a moment I see a tinge of pity

in her eyes. Pity was something I had become all too familiar with over the years. She shoves it aside quick before answering me. "I'm not sure. I suppose some things in life should be experienced firsthand."

Her comment wasn't meant to be harsh, but I could sense the simplicity her words meant to deliver. Both of them made life appear effortless. If only I could have a fraction of that ease. To walk down Main Street with confidence in my step. To talk to strangers without my heart racing in my chest or my limbs trembling. To have some semblance of normalcy.

What I wouldn't give for an ounce of their strength and courage.

Lena cajoles me—her best pouty lips and puppy dog eyes on display. "Come on, Mags. Let loose a little with us tonight. It'll be good for you. I promise. You know we'd never let anything happen to you."

They were doing what they thought best for me. Trying to help me tear down the wall I'd built around myself years ago. Helping me to grow again, in a different way than our youth. Bringing out the beauty they saw in me, allowing it to blossom. To discover the newer version of myself.

I want to be free from my past. More than anything.

But fear floods my veins. No matter how brave I want to be, it still holds me captive. A vicious cycle of freedom and restriction.

I trust Lessa and Lena with my life. They would never put me in harm's way. I wish they knew how to extinguish the anxiety pinning me down. To vanquish the uneasiness holding me back from the world.

How does one overcome fear?

How can I escape and discover everything I have been missing?

How do I open myself up to new possibilities?

Introspective for a few minutes, Lessa and Lena continue a quiet conversation between themselves, allowing me time to think. My quiet tendencies have never been odd to them, not since Mom died.

My fingers fidget with the silverware on my napkin while my thoughts wage war inside my head. It would be great to do something fun with them, for a change.

It had been so long since *fun* had been a word in my vocabulary. I miss fun.

Plus, their judgment had never been something I questioned or doubted.

Taking a deep breath, I speak with hesitancy, "Okay, I'm in for going upstairs." As I say the words, butterflies flutter with intensity in my belly. *Deep breath in, deep breath out. I can do this.*

Lessa shrieks, and it surprises me the whole restaurant didn't turn to shush her. "Yes! We're going to have the best time up there. I can feel it in my bones."

Although I couldn't match her exuberance, I express myself the only way I know how. With loads of awkwardness. I raise my glass and smile. "Here's to being myself, living outside the box, and diving in headfirst."

CHAPTER 2

GEOFFREY

Time crept at a snail's pace, the day never ending. Arriving at work earlier than usual, I have spent the last ten hours putting the finishing touches on my part of the Hair of The Dog Tavern project—a new dog-friendly bar opening in town.

My business partners dubbed *perfection* as my middle name, joking at how antsy I became when I neared the end of a project. I gave them the middle finger—a gesture of my love for them.

Is it a crime to want everything in the right place before it left my hands?

For some reason, it was joke-worthy.

What wasn't funny were the continuous interruptions while I was engrossed in my work.

Excuse me, sir. You have a call.

Hey, Geoff. Can I talk to you for a moment?

I'm headed to lunch. You want to tag along?

Everyone was doing their job or extending courtesy and I couldn't fault them. But when I had a deadline approaching, unless the building was on fire, I couldn't deal with the constant interruptions.

Sometimes I wondered if the friends and employees I worked with knew me well at all. If they did, they'd know to leave me to my solitude while I finish the last leg of my work.

Or perhaps they did know and they were fucking with me on purpose. *Dicks.*

After countless hours and many sleepless nights, elation spreads from my chest throughout my body. The paperwork on my desk is nothing short of perfection and I wouldn't have it any other way.

I roll the drawings up, the papers crinkling as I tap the ends even, then slide them into the cardboard tube. Each time I cap the end of a new tube, I get a little burst of energy, knowing I'm helping shape Lake Lavender.

As I stand, my chair whooshes across the floor behind me. After snagging my jacket from the back of the chair, I press the power off on my monitor. As I'm grabbing my keys and phone off the credenza, a knock raps on my office door.

Logan stands in the archway, leaning on the frame. "Hey, man. You get everything squared away today?"

"I did. Thanks for checking on me, Mom," I joke. "The drawings look phenomenal. I wanted everything finished today, so I wouldn't think about it over the weekend. Now, I can have a weekend for the first time in months."

"Fricking work porn," he mumbles, rolling his eyes.

"Idiot," I retort, laughing at our usual banter.

Logan walks over and slaps me hard on my upper back. "That's great, bro. I'm proud of you. Finished a week early. Is that the reason behind your shit-eating grin?"

I swear he lives and breathes to fuck with me. Continuing

to collect my things, I ignore him. He'll continue in three, two, one...

"You tell Owen yet?"

Called it.

"I planned to tell him before heading out. And as for this," I say, pointing at the non-fading smile, "I expect I'll see something similar plastered on your face when you finish. So, don't be a dick."

He loves razzing me as much as I do him. The day it stops, we'd both know something wasn't right.

"Whatever, man. You headed home for the night?"

"I thought I'd go out and have a drink or two to celebrate finishing things early. You have any plans?"

"No plans. You mind if I tag along? I could use a drink and some visual stimulus before going home," he pauses when I hold my hand up, a brief moment of TMI. "We need to go out more often. We're turning into old men here," he laughs out.

"You know I don't mind. I hadn't thought of where to go yet. Any ideas?" I ask. "I only have one stipulation. It has to be somewhere we can sit down, enjoy our drinks and not get bumped by obnoxious crowds."

As high on cloud nine as I was, I wanted to wind down and enjoy the bliss coursing through me.

"Give me a minute to grab my things. Go talk with Owen and see if he wants to go with us. I know he hasn't been out in a while. I swear he's the workaholic version of a monk. Always in his office or house and glued to the damn computer," he smirks.

I chuckle at the thought, knowing we each zone out when we're working. Owen just happens to be married to his career.

"Cool. I'll meet you out front in a few."

Flipping the light off in my office, I laugh to myself as I head to Owen's office.

Logan wasn't wrong; Owen behaved like an outcast. Hands down, he dedicated his life to work. But work-life balance was essential. Work and sleep were not the only two things in life.

After bantering with Owen a few minutes, I win our little debate and he agrees to go out. This moment should be recorded for posterity.

Stepping outside, we join Logan as he waits for us.

The Architectural Crimson building is less than luxurious, but has more of an artistic and modern vibe. The front entrance is floor to ceiling glass, while the remainder of the building has a warehouse feel. Slate tile covers the floors. A black and gray rug dominating the waiting area floor. The furniture simplistic and minimal, showing clients less can be more.

Portfolios loaded with images of our projects sit on resin-coated wood tables—the wood an actual slice of tree. Sculptures, paintings and murals, glass and woodwork; all available for purchase, minus the murals.

Each of us contributed to the energy and appearance, the same as our projects. It's important our clients understand the type of architectural and design firm they're working with as they stepped through our front door. That they saw our personalities, tastes, and layouts firsthand.

And every time a client complimented our work, my heart beats a little faster.

"Where do you want to go, man? This is your rodeo," Logan prompts.

"It's been too damn long since I've gone out on a Friday

night," I say. "The only two places that fit the bill are Black Silk and On Tap. One of you pick. Either is good with me."

Surprising both of us, Owen speaks up first.

"Let's go to Black Silk. We haven't stepped foot in there for a year. It'd be great to see how business is going for Cheryl."

"Good evening, Mr. Lawson. What brings the three of you here this evening?" Cheryl's greeting is as warm as malt liquor as she embraces each of us in turn.

Cheryl has been our most challenging client to date.

She never nitpicked our work or threw out impossible deadlines. She never asked inane questions or gave crazy demands. No, the challenge she presented was a creative one. One that taxed our ingenuity and sometimes tested our integrity. Cheryl herself was a sight to behold too, testing our professionalism.

Frequently.

But looking was the extent of my actions. For Logan and Owen too. The tall, elegant blonde was a client, a savvy businesswoman we respected, and a successful business owner in the community who bragged about our work. She was off limits.

"Hey, Cheryl. We just completed the first phase of a new project. It calls for a night out."

"That's wonderful news. I assume all is running smooth, as usual." Excitement for us evident in her tone. "Did you want a table, the bar, or planning to head upstairs?"

Facing Logan and Owen, I tilt my head in question. Both give me the same benign shrug. "Upstairs sounds great, Cheryl. Has it been busy tonight?"

"I've seen a decent crowd head up, but it won't pick up for another hour or two."

Heading toward the walkway off to our right, we were more than ready to unwind. "Perfect. Thanks, Cheryl," I call over my shoulder. "We'll be sure to catch you before we leave."

Logan and Owen in tow, she waved us away, telling us to enjoy our evening.

The dim light from the dining area lit the banister. I ran a hand over the lacquered honey oak. The hand-carved, intricate lines feel like braille under my fingertips. The swirl of the grain creating a unique pattern matching no other.

But at the top of the stairs, the walls transition from charcoal to burgundy. And the atmosphere shifts as well. We are no longer in the elegant dining space. A new energy pulses in the air, desire taking hold of the space surrounding us.

Artwork fills the length of the hall leading to the nightclub's entrance, just as it did the walls in the dining area. Except the art on these walls has more edge and desire— hands, mouths, bodies. Each drawing, painting or photograph is meant to stimulate the onlooker.

They're not necessarily meant to arouse, although a few stirred the bulge in my pants. They're meant to open the mind to new experiences. Experiences like those beyond the door of the nightclub.

A muscular, intimidating man verifies our identification, grants us access and wishes us a good evening, the tally tracker in his left hand clicking three times as we enter. The last time we stepped inside these walls, a building inspector stood beside us, lights brightening every inch of the space.

Tonight, every aspect is a new experience. Tonight, everything about this place is alive and energized.

Maneuvering through the crowd, we pass an open mahogany space in the center of the room. Bodies gyrating to the music, sweat penetrating cotton and blending with others' skin.

Low tables, constructed from the same pale oak as those in the restaurant, surround the dance floor. Candles at the center add a soft, dim light and a subtle vanilla aroma. Beside each table sits a black-framed, oxblood leather couch. Warm light diffuses from the crown molding above the bar opposite the entrance.

Logan, Owen, and I sit on black wooden stools at the end of the bar. Less than a minute passes and a young blonde woman with smoky eyes and a red smile greets us.

"Good evening, gentlemen. What can I get for you to drink tonight?"

With a petite frame and a curvaceous body, she is eye-catching. But she isn't my type.

Logan, on the other hand, has a liking for blondes. No doubt he is already plotting how to leave with her number.

We each order our drink of choice, sitting in silence a minute after the bartender walks off.

As soon as she is out of earshot, Logan's restraint falls. "I'd like to be the first to say… she is easy on the eyes."

I roll my eyes at Logan and try my damnedest to not laugh. So predictable.

Behind the bar, only one other bartender is working tonight, a guy who must hit the gym on a regular basis. No doubt the majority of his clientele is female.

As I'm sure most of our bartender's clients are male. I also don't doubt they'll flirt with the same sex, if the vibe of the patron leans that way.

She sets our drinks in front of us and departs. Logan, still stuck in high school, watches her backside as she moves behind the bar.

He looks over to me and asks, "So, what are my chances, man? Do you think a woman *that* hot will give her number before we leave?"

Fortunately for Owen, he learned years ago to ignore Logan when the subject of women was the topic of choice. He mastered the art of avoidance, an avoidance he displays while sipping his beer.

Me? Somehow, I became his wingman and guidance counselor. "What chance do *you* think you have? I've given up on guessing that shit. When it comes to you, people surprise me time and again."

Logan feigns a punch to my arm, calling me an asshole.

Bunching my eyebrows, I force out a huff and mock-rub my arm.

Laughs erupt from our small section of the bar and it is exactly what we needed tonight. Laughter and a night away from the monotony.

The sea of bodies has grown in the few minutes we've been here, now filling the four walls. Some sitting alone on couches, eyes glued to cell phones. Others lounging on the leather couches, sipping on their alcohol of choice and chatting with friends.

As I make a last visual circuit of the room, I catch sight of a brunette. My eyes lock on her frame, my breath trapped in my lungs.

She is stunning. Maybe five-and-a-half feet tall. Long, chocolate locks a juxtaposition to her creamy skin.

Two women stand on either side of her, dancing carefree and coaxing her to join. But she stands there, her frame closing in on itself and her hands fidgeting at her sides.

A light strobes across the darkened dance floor, high-lighting the fear in her eyes, as if she's silently screaming to leave. Bodies grind beside her and she cringes. As each second passes, she becomes more panic-stricken.

Rhythm and bass pulse around me, but it's no comparison to the forceful thumping behind my ribcage.

Owen and Logan are deep in conversation. Neither pays me attention as I retrieve my phone, acting like just another schlub glued to his email. Instead, I open the camera and capture an image of her. In the dim light of the club, and with no flash, the picture is grainy.

I stare at the photo, comparing its model with the real thing every few seconds, and guilt resonates in my gut. Does this picture classify me as a creep? Yes. Do I care? No.

It has been more than a decade since I was enthralled by a woman. Entranced beyond a simple distraction. Who could compare to Charlotte? The thought jumpstarts my heart and has me gasping for breath.

Is it time?

Pushing the uncomfortable thought aside, I watch as she brushes her hair away from her face. I wish it were my fingers fulfilling the action.

When she resists her friends' attempts to get her dancing, I want to rise from my stool and walk over to her and wrap my arms around her waist, find her a quiet nook where she can relax the way she so obviously needs to.

But she is walking off the dance floor before I can move, the sway of her hips suggestive but her expression saying some-thing different as she sits down.

She watches her friends enjoy themselves, a glint in her eye. Envy, maybe?

Could this woman be the distraction I've needed? Months

have come and gone since I've had a woman beneath me. Too many months. I could use a female distraction in my life.

But isn't she more?

No. No one will ever be *more*.

Emotions are never a part of the equation anymore. Desire, lust, cravings. That is all I need. All I can allow. And right now, desire has me wanting to meet this woman. The hunger rests low in my groin, bulging below my zipper. Her magnetism is foreign and unwelcome, but I'm resigned to one decision.

No matter what, before either of us leaves here tonight, I will know her name.

CHAPTER 3
MAGDALENA

I'm suffocating.

I've never been in a bar, let alone a nightclub. Friday nights with Lessa and Lena consisted of dinner and idle chitchat. Always simple. Always familiar.

When I agreed to come here, I thought I'd be surrounded by people barely old enough to drink. I was wrong. From what I can see, the place isn't crawling with immaturity or people looking for an easy hook-up, but rather with mixed crowd. White- and blue-collared people winding down and letting go of their inhibitions. College age individuals in graphic t-shirts and jeans laugh, dance, and catch up. Groups of women enjoying a lady's night out, dressed to the nines and primped as if they just left the salon.

But I am surrounded.

As prepared as I thought I'd be, the mass of people now surrounding me wipes my strength away. There is no personal space. No respect for boundaries. But retreating to a couch alone for solitude brings on a new level of discomfort.

At one end of the bar, a man watches me, his stare evident.

Not wanting the attention, I play cool and continue my scan of the club before returning my eyes to the table in front of me.

Making the dance floor my focal point, I watch Lessa and Lena while keeping the bar in my periphery. But the man still stares. Paranoia seeps in my consciousness, rearing its ugly head.

After I've been visually stalked for minutes that feel like hours, Lena and Lessa return from the dance floor. Out of breath, a thin layer of sweat on their skin, they both plop on the couch, laughing. A twinge of jealousy squeezes my heart, and I wish enjoying life was as easy for me as it is them.

After she catches her breath, Lessa asks, "How are you feeling, Mags? You had me scared for a moment out there."

As always, everyone is concerned about poor, little Magdalena. This is why I want normal. Why I need it.

"I'm better now," I tell her. "I'm just a bit overwhelmed. Tonight has been packed with new experiences. More than I've handled in years. But I'm okay. Promise."

I lean against the back of the couch, the coolness of the leather piercing my top and erasing a layer of heat from my body. With the two of them at my side, I'm able to relax more.

Lena pops up from the couch. "I'm going to grab us all water. Be right back." And before I can thank her, she vanishes in the crowd.

The weight of my secret admirer stirs in my belly. As Lessa rambles on about loving the music, I nod on occasion but don't hear a word she says. I can't confirm without him knowing, but I feel his eyes continuing to watch me. His heat boring into me.

When Lena returns, half my water disappears before I set the glass down.

My voice a fraction above the music, I profess, "I don't want either of you to be obvious after what I say next. Okay?"

A quizzical expression pops up on each of their faces, both of them nodding in agreement.

"Over at the bar, there's a man who has been staring at me for at least ten minutes. Without seeming obvious, look at the end of the bar and tell me if he's still staring."

We talk on the couch, random things creating our conversation while each of them searched for him. After endless faux conversation, Lena stops mentioning the week's forecast. Her eyes halting for a split-second before resuming their scan of the space.

She sees him.

"If you are referring to the tall, handsome guy. Hair about chin length, in a suit... Then, yes. I'd say he's staring his way into your soul."

And like the flick of a switch, my anxiety reignites.

"I think I'm going to call it a night, ladies. As fun as some parts of tonight have been, this has become far too overwhelming for my blood."

I take one last drink of water from my glass, tuck my clutch under my arm, and rise from the couch. Without a doubt, I have stepped way outside of my comfort zone tonight.

Guilt engulfs me for wanting to leave already, but I don't foresee the evening getting better. "I'm really sorry. Maybe we can try this again. Next Friday, perhaps?" I hate myself for being the Debbie Downer. "Tonight was a little much. I'm sure next time will be better. Forgive me?"

They shake their heads, soft laughter escaping their lips. Neither of them is disappointed in my wanting to leave—their smiles tell me as much.

"Go home, Mags. We'll see you later. Love you!" Lessa tells me, jumping up to wrap me in her arms.

When she releases me from her bear hug, I give Lena a hug goodbye. "I love you both. I'll text you guys tomorrow. Enjoy the club for me."

Heading for the exit, I weave through a dozen people standing near the wall, my head tilted forward. As I'm about to pass the person in front of me, he veers in the same direction and stops me. Shifting my attention from the floor, ready to ask the man to let me pass, all thought vanishes.

It's the guy from the bar.

Standing inches from me and blocking my path.

My heart hammers against my ribcage as my breath catches. And for a moment, I forget how to function like a human.

"Excuse me, I'm trying to leave," I mutter, pointing toward the exit.

My eyes level with his chest, a crisp, white dress shirt with a dark tie consumes my view. Just above his collar is a sprinkling of blond stubble. He doesn't budge and I squirm before him.

I tip my head back and follow the scruff-covered line of his jaw. When I reach his eyes, breathing becomes a distant memory.

Striking, crystalline, Caribbean blue eyes study my face. My eyes refuse to leave his, not that I'm making an effort.

My shoulders relax as I memorize my new favorite shade of blue. Every ounce of discomfort from his voyeurism fades away. A new, unfamiliar emotion takes hold. Ease and solace swirl in my chest.

Whatever this is, I'm curious enough to not stray.

He leans into me, his lips a breath from my ear. A sweet,

earthy scent fills my nose. "Hi, I'm Geoff. I noticed you a little bit ago on the dance floor. You looked like you'd seen a ghost. I wanted to see if you were okay."

Disappointment twists my heart, my shoulders slumping as a sigh escapes my lips. One more person to add to the list, everyone always worrying over Magdalena. For once, it would be nice for someone to not be concerned over me. For once, it would be nice to have a normal conversation.

"I'm fine, thank you. I'm calling it a night. I appreciate your concern, but you have no need to worry. If you'll excuse me."

I shuffle to my right to step around him, but he shifts at the same time and blocks the exit. "I apologize if I come off as rude, it's not my intent. I wanted to come over sooner and introduce myself." He glances to the side for three heartbeats before returning his eyes to mine, his lips parted in unspoken thought. "I also wanted to ask if you were seeing someone. And if not, would you like to go out sometime? I realize that's forward of me, but I had to ask before you left."

I freeze in place—everything but my jaw, which drops. No doubt I look broken. Like an idiot unable to answer a simple question. My initial hesitancy nothing to do with his demeanor or approaching me, but the fact he just asked me out on a date.

And yet there isn't an ounce of discomfort answering his question, which is strange. I don't know this man, yet I want to tell him everything. But part of me resists, my inner fortress yelling at me to keep my guard intact.

"Thank you for the apology, it's much appreciated. As for the other question, that's rather personal—and I don't know you. Now, if you'll excuse me…"

I step to the left this time, but once again he mimics my movement. If my shoulders could hit the floor in defeat, it's a guarantee that's where I'd find them. I meet his ocean-colored eyes and beg him to let me pass.

His hands come up in surrender, sincerity in his expression. His lips part, then pinch tight before he leans into me again. His teakwood scent encompasses me and I breathe deep.

"Please forgive me. But can you answer one question before you leave?"

My cheek grazes his collar as I nod.

"I'd like to know the name of the woman who has held me captive for the last hour."

That's it? My name?

If giving this man my name was all he wanted, what was the harm? It's just a name. And there's only so much you can do with a name.

So I acquiesce, my voice timid as his breath continues to heat my neck. "Magdalena. My name is Magdalena."

He leans away from me and I exhale, not realizing I've been holding my breath since I caught his scent. I squeeze past him, our bodies brushing against each other for a half second, a buzz lingering from the contact.

My feet have a mind of their own as I speed walk the hall and down the stairs. Once I step outside, I drag in a deep breath and make a beeline for my car.

My path from the club to my car is a blur.

I crank the ignition and grip the wheel until my knuckles are white. *Deep breath in, deep breath out.*

The whooshing of my blood echoes behind my ears, dizziness on the cusp of returning. But it's not like it was earlier. Earlier, it was the music and the crowd and the intense atmosphere. This... it was *him*.

Turning a dial on the dash to the far right, a burst of cold air brings some relief. I aim all the vents in my direction and drop my forehead to the steering wheel.

My head swims with emotion. Thoughts overflowing and spilling on the ground. One question runs a continual cycle in the foreground.

Why did I leave?

And that single question… it scares me the most.

CHAPTER 4

GEOFFREY

After living in this house for five years, I have never noticed the ceiling above my bed is textured. Until tonight.

My eyes haven't left the ceiling in hours. My mind busy creating fantasies. Daydreaming of Magdalena. Depriving me of sleep and dreams.

Dreamland—a place where my brain can go wild with thoughts of her. Of us. Of what could be.

A loud grumble interrupts the silence in the room. Rumbling again, I rub my stomach to calm my hunger. I hadn't realized until this moment, but lunch was the last time I'd eaten. Regardless, I have zero desire to leave my bed. It is far too late, or too early, to eat.

One thought rang on repeat, overriding everything else.

Magdalena.

I wanted to drift off and dream all things her.

The curves of her body and sway of her hips. The way her eyes peeked up at mine and how her lips formed words as she

When she stood from the couch and grabbed her purse, I rose off my stool. Logan and Owen shot me a look, wondering why I'd bolted upright. I gave them a tale and told them I thought I saw an old friend. They resumed drinking and talking while I zigzagged to the exit as fast as my feet would move.

When she stopped in front of me, every nerve ending in my body fired.

With most women, their body was what attracted me. But Magdalena is different.

Yes, my blood heated when I caught a glimpse of her contours. Any man who enjoyed the company of a woman would have reacted the same. With a buxom frame, my fingers itched to touch her.

But her proximity stole my breath.

Did she detect my reaction? Was her pulse as erratic as mine?

Flashes of her dark locks and glossed, plump lips dance behind my eyelids.

Oh, how I'd love to taste those lips.

The memory of her subtle rosy scent hits the air as if she were next to me again.

A moan disrupts my silent bedroom.

Magdalena would be a recurring guest star in my dreams for the foreseeable future. It had been a while since I dreamt of a woman. Charlotte was the last woman to consume me in this way. Perhaps it has just been too long since my last distraction.

My body screams for me to satiate my physical urges, while my mind speaks calm words regarding relationships and courting. But since Charlotte, dating has never evolved into anything serious. Distractions and sex were all that sustained me. All I would allow.

I didn't want love. Or to hand over my heart.

Because when I lost Charlotte, it felt like those parts of me left with her.

Tick. Tock. Tick. Tock.

The wall clock from the living room continues ticking away and I have yet to fall asleep. I sneak a glance at the clock on my bedside table and note the time. Three-seventeen.

Nothing regarding the hours passing shocks me. But with the sunrise looming in the distance, I can't lie here awake all night. Sleep was necessary.

I'd resemble the walking dead tomorrow if I didn't at least get five hours of sleep. And tomorrow—well today—I'd need my wits about me if I planned to be productive. Because tomorrow I had one goal.

Find Magdalena.

The next morning, Black Silk seems the most logical place to start. Cheryl or one of her staff are bound to remember seeing her.

Although they don't open to the public for hours, I know staff are already busy inside preparing for the evening.

I press the disguised doorbell to the left of the doors, the button reserved for visitors during non-business hours, and wait. A minute later, the door cracks open. A man pushes the door open wider, smiles, and gestures for me to enter.

Once inside, Cheryl approaches me, curiosity written in her expression. I school my features, mentally rehearsing my strategy, and attempt to disguise wiping my hands over the backside of my jeans as tucking them in the pockets.

"How lucky am I to see you twice in twenty-four hours? That hasn't happened since we opened."

We exchange a brief hug. *Wrong height, wrong frame.* The stray thought has me releasing the embrace sooner than expected.

"I know, right? I hope I'm not intruding." I pause, schooling my tone to something like polite concern. "Do you mind if I ask you something?"

She leans on the hostess podium, regarding me with interest. "Of course, I don't mind. What's up?"

"There was a woman in the club last night and I wanted to see if you knew her. I bumped her, on accident, and she was gone before I could apologize. I spilled my drink on her and I'd like the opportunity to pay for any cleaning bill she may have."

There was little truth in my words, but Cheryl didn't need to be privy to my baby white lie. Spilling my drink was the most *valid* reason I'd come up with on my way here.

Cheryl's expression twists into something unreadable. She tips her head to one side, her eyes tight as she assesses me. We stand like this—neither of us moving—for a moment. As each second passes, my chance at answers slips away. Did Cheryl see through my fib? *Fuck, I hope not.*

"You bumped into her on *accident*? That doesn't sound like something you'd do, Geoff."

Doubt and questioning. I am so fucked.

She has to know something is off, but can't place it. Her pinched brows and eyes say everything her mouth doesn't. Any second now, the interrogation would start. Cheryl's intelligence is one of her attractive qualities, but not in the current situation.

Resigning to the fact this is a no-win situation, I surrender. "It's alright. I wanted to be a gentleman and pay for my mistake. I'm sure I'll see her somewhere around town."

When I turn away, my frame deflates a fraction. Two steps forward and her slender fingers wrap around my forearm, stopping me. Hope reignites in my chest, but I conceal it from displaying on my face.

"Hey, I'm sorry. Most men aren't looking to be polite; they're looking to hook up. It happens often, guys asking the staff about women. It's my responsibility to look out for everyone that walks through my doors, especially the women. You understand, right?" she pleads, her brow furrowed as she gazes at me.

Guilt wraps around my torso and squeezes like a too-tight bandage. *Am I one of those guys?* Maybe.

"Cheryl, I would never do anything to hurt you or your business. I hope you believe that. In some respects, this is my business, too."

"I know. It's just instinctual for me to be defensive with situations like this, regardless who's asking. Again, I'm sorry. What can you tell me about the woman? I can't guarantee I know her, but maybe some of the staff will."

My first opportunity to discover more about Magdalena has my palms sweating. I need to be as subtle as possible. Phrase my inquiry the right way. Be careful with my choice of words. Limit any further suspicion on my part. After what Cheryl just said to me, if I appear like "one of those guys", I will be digging my own grave.

"Thanks, Cheryl. I appreciate you helping. She looked to be in her mid-twenties. A darker brunette. She was wearing a dark top, maybe black, and white pants. I believe I saw her with two other women and overheard one say Magdalena, but I can't be certain that's her."

"Give me a minute, I'll go check with the staff who worked last night. Be right back."

I lean against a thick wooden post as Cheryl heads for the staff service area. It's odd to see Black Silk after all this time. Although our firm placed every piece of furniture, was responsible for most of its appearance, it didn't look quite the same. Like it was no longer an infant, but was reaching those toddler years.

A few minutes later, she returns. Her face gives nothing away. But I also can't try to force anything out of her. It would reveal my desperation. And the fact I lied to her about my reason for being here.

"Okay, so here's what I've been told. The woman you described as Magdalena has been in the restaurant maybe two or three times with two other women, but they come on Fridays. Last night was the first time they went into the club. Their server last night said the other two are named Lessa and Lena. They were at their table for close to two hours before entering the club. He doesn't remember much else, sorry. I wish I could tell you more." Her face falls.

"Thank you for asking around. I promise I'll find a way to repay you. And please, stop pouting as if you lost your puppy," I tease. "I'll figure something out. Even if I have to return next Friday, that's better than nothing." I muster up a half smile. "I hope we can all catch up sometime soon. You can update us on how business is going."

"It's a date. Sort of," she laughs. She wraps an arm around my neck, pulling me in for one last hug before we part ways.

As I exit the restaurant and walk to my car, a strange funk slithers through my body. I had zero expectations going in, but I hoped to find out more than her friends' names. The information is more than I had walked in with, but it's still a letdown.

What the hell could I do with names? It's not like I could walk around town asking citizens if they knew any of the three women. I'd be locked up in jail within minutes as some creepy stalker. And that wasn't happening.

I'd hit a wall. A dead end.

Defeat rested on my shoulder like a wicked devil, laughing in my ear at my failure. I need a pick me up. Something to give me a boost and get my brain firing on all cylinders. Maybe I could come up with some other plan, a different way to approach the situation.

I drive around town a few minutes before parking next to my new favorite coffee shop. When problems need solving, caffeine is the answer. Food an added bonus.

A bell jingles on the door as I open it, the barista behind the counter looking up at me.

"Welcome to Java & Teas Me," the young woman hollers, her voice bubbly.

I've been here twice now and love the non-chain vibe. Local women own the small business, but I have yet to meet them. Whoever they are, they have impeccable taste.

The walls are littered with artwork by local artists. No two pieces are the same medium, and each calls out to someone different. The vibe is laid back, patrons laughing and enjoying themselves. Teens and college-age kids occupy the different size tables, as well as young professionals. There is even an area off to the side with over-sized bean bag chairs and end tables.

As I approach the counter, the woman who greets me is all smiles.

I order a black coffee and a BEATS ME sandwich—bacon, egg, avocado, tomato, sprouts, and muenster cheese on an English muffin.

I sit at a small table toward the back corner, setting my order number card on the table, my isolation a reflection of my current mood. My failure still fresh in my thoughts, I wallow in my misery. I'm still irritated my search ended as quickly as it began.

The blended aroma of bacon and cheese disrupts me from shredding the napkin I pulled from the holder. A second later, a plate tinkers against the constellation-lacquered table in front of me.

I turn to the woman delivering my food to thank her—and am speechless. It isn't the young woman who took my order minutes earlier. Smiling in front of me is one of the women I saw with Magdalena in Black Silk.

I sit frozen, gawking at her, and make this moment awkward and uncomfortable for us both. The probability of this very moment happening is slim to none. I take it as a sign or fate or whatever term you want to throw at it. How can I not?

"Is something the matter, sir? You ordered the BEATS ME sandwich, correct?" She lifts the ticket in her hand, comparing it to the card number on the table.

"Yes, yes. Sorry about that. It's just... you look familiar, that's all. I didn't mean to space out. Just having one of those déjà vu moments. Do I know you from somewhere?" Knowing full well where I have seen her, I play my card. Does she remember me?

"I don't recall meeting you before, but I do meet quite a number of people by owning a coffee shop. My name's Alessandra, but most people call me Lessa. And you are?" Her hand extends in my direction and I shake it.

Confirmation.

She's a few inches taller than Magdalena, her dark blonde hair secured in a tight ponytail. She looks about the same age as Magdalena—and friendly enough to be my in.

Lessa is a vault of knowledge. I just need the tools to break her open.

"Hi, I'm Geoff. It's nice to meet you, Lessa. I've been here a couple times after hearing all the rave reviews. I don't recall meeting you on my previous visits though." I pause, pondering a moment how to proceed. Snapping my fingers, I continue. "Wait a second. A couple guys from work and I went out last night. Black Silk. Maybe that's where I've seen you?" I leave a hint of doubt in my voice.

Even so, my question weighs heavy in the air, her silence making me leery as I wait for her to confirm what I already know.

"I was there last night, with a couple of girlfriends. I don't remember seeing you, though." Confusion and reluctance furrow her brow.

There I go again, putting the damn cart before the horse. Shit.

Slow the hell down and back up.

She probably thinks I'm some psycho stalker—not that I'm far off at this point. At least my intentions aren't creepy.

"My friends and I had a couple celebratory drinks after finishing part of a project at the office. We were at the bar and I must've skimmed past you while people watching. I hadn't been in since it opened, so I was eager to check everything out."

Her shoulders relax as she takes a deep breath. "Oh, okay. Last night was the first time we'd been in the club. It's amazing. At the top of my favorites list now."

The urge to continue talking rides me. I need to keep her talking, too. Perhaps she would volunteer more information if I gave some up first.

"My architectural firm designed the building and assisted

with the development of the interior. It's a favorite of ours, as well. Cheryl, the owner, had a specific vision for her business and was great at implementing it."

Lessa's mouth pops open. "Oh, wow! Are you Geoff Lawson? Of Architectural Crimson?"

Wait, she knows *my* name? Had we met before last night? Queasiness tightens my gut. Shit. "I am. How did you know?" Generally, I'm good with remembering names and faces. And neither spark a memory when it comes to this woman.

"I read about your company in the paper before I opened the coffee shop. I'd love to sit down with you all sometime and pick your brains about some ideas I had for the café."

Well, this conversation took a turn I wasn't expecting. "What is there to talk about? This place is amazing and a much-preferred destination over the other options available."

A smile lights up her face. "Thanks! We don't want to change the vibe of the shop, but there are some structural changes we'd like done. We have somewhat of an idea of what we want to change and how we want things to look, but that's not our area of expertise. I mean, what do we know about structural safety and integrity or if it's even possible to do what we're thinking?"

Although I knew the shop was owned by a few local women, I had never researched who. No valid reason prompted me to do so. "Who is we?" A sneaking suspicion threads its way through my bloodstream, leaving adrenaline in its wake. But I don't want to assume. I need to hear the truth with my own ears.

"Oh yes, I'm sorry. The shop is owned by myself and my two friends, Helena and Magdalena. I run the shop for the most part. They're more like silent partners. But whenever important decisions are made—financial or development—we make them together. They both have other jobs, but help out here when absolutely necessary."

I'm soaring high in the clouds now, singing of sweet victory after finding this significant piece to the Magdalena puzzle. I could find out even more about her, now that I know she is a partial owner of the coffee shop.

But as quick as I soar, I plummet again.

If a business contract was written up with us and the coffee shop, it would nix any opportunity for me to have a personal relationship with Magdalena. Because if there was one rule Owen, Logan, and I were adamant about, it was not mixing business and pleasure.

This can't be the end. Not when we haven't had a beginning.

There has to be a beginning.

An idea strikes like lightning.

"Thank you for considering us in regards to the coffee shop, but we generally build from scratch. You have a fantastic structure already in place and clientele who love the place as it is. May I make some recommendations for other companies that could assist you in what I believe you're looking for?"

Her shoulders slump forward and she appears crestfallen. But she masks it well when she responds. "What would the difference be between what you offer and this other company you'd recommend? No offense to the other company, but I want things done to a certain standard and won't take anything less."

Wow. She strikes me speechless by her compliment, my cheeks pained from the smile it evokes.

"Thank you. I would never recommend anyone I didn't trust. Plus, you're just seeking a few small structural changes, not starting from the ground up. I can refer you to the proper people and they will do what you're wanting. I promise you.

I'll even give you my business card and if they aren't keeping you happy with what they propose or do, you call me."

This appeases her. The evidence written in the relaxing of her brow and her fade-resistant smile. When it came to business, I didn't play games and would never associate myself with anyone who did. The integrity of our business was of utmost importance, as well as customer satisfaction.

Now that I had an 'in' with Magdalena's friend, Alessandra, I decide to propose an inquiry about her friends.

"So, if all three of you own the café, but you run it by yourself, what do your partners do for work outside of here?"

Her lack of hesitation to answer gratifying, as I had made our conversation and relationship more comfortable in the last five minutes.

"Helena owns and runs a local boutique shop, Always Classic. She sells vintage-looking apparel and accessories and whatnot. Magdalena is a full-time volunteer counselor at Statice, the youth center assisting children with no living family."

I stumble back mentally, at a loss for words. I suppose Magdalena receives income from Java and Teas Me. But volunteering full-time says a lot regarding someone's character. And their upbringing.

What happened in her life to make her dedicate so much time to helping others?

Lessa snaps me out of my train of thought when she touches my arm.

"I'm sorry, I didn't mean to interrupt your day off. And I've probably let your food get cold, too. I can make you another, if you'd like?"

I shook my head. "No, that's okay. You should get back to work before the staff starts losing it. It was a pleasure to meet you, Lessa."

"Me too. I look forward to meeting with the other company you're referring me. Thank you." She juts her hand forward, shaking mine. I hand her my business card after jotting down the other company's information on the back.

A smile filling her cheeks, she turns away from me and heads for the kitchen, out of my view.

As soon as I felt no eyes on me, I bask in the plethora of information I have learned. My mind held Magdalena's secret as if it were the most precious thing in the world. Because it was.

At least it was for me.

CHAPTER 5
MAGDALENA

I squint, temporarily blinded as I walk out the tinted glass doors of Statice. Stopping outside the doors, I dig through my purse and search for my sunglasses. As soon as I slip them in place, I make a beeline for my little black car.

Today was rough at the center. Whenever a new child walks through the door, it's never an easy day.

The first meeting with Jason keeps replaying in my head. Watching a thirteen-year-old boy breakdown in tears from heartbreak; it's devastating. His father passed away due to a heart problem the family was unaware of. His mother didn't respond well to the loss of her husband and has been admitted to a psychiatric facility for an indefinite period of time.

Although each case is different, I do my damnedest to let them know they still have people who care about them. And that they have a support system anytime they need one. Statice offered me the same support, not so many years ago.

Fifteen feet from my car, I get an overwhelming feeling I'm being followed. It's not something I'm familiar with, but there's no other way to describe it. Slowing my pace, I side glance at the rear window of the car closest to me. My breath hitches when I catch the reflection of a masculine figure behind me.

He's in jeans and a navy button-down shirt, the sleeves rolled to his elbows. As I focus my attention forward, I hear his footsteps increase in speed and volume.

As I hurry to my car, I berate myself for not having my keys in hand. As a single woman, being prepared and vigilant are vital. No matter how many times I have lectured myself regarding the subject, I have yet to break the habit.

Stopping next to my driver's side door, my hand dives into my purse. When a warmth lands on my shoulder, I jump away from the contact and shriek.

I pivot, my heart racing a marathon in my chest, my lungs panting for fresh air. But as soon as I lock eyes with a set of Caribbean blue eyes, the worry I had moments ago is replaced with relief. And curiosity.

His hands lift in surrender as his brow furrows. "Hey, hey, hey. I didn't mean to scare you, Magdalena. Are you alright?"

I hold up a finger. "Hi," I huff, resting a hand over my erratic heart. "I'll be fine in a minute. You scared me half to death. Geoff, right?" I pause and allow my lungs to settle as he nods. "Why are you following me? You aren't some type of weirdo stalker, are you?"

My brain to mouth filter must be on hiatus. Regardless, I didn't care. *Who is this guy?* The more important question... *why the hell is he following me?*

Laughter breaks the awkwardness floating in the air between us. Part of me soothed by the sound, another part of me remains hesitant.

"No, Magdalena, I'm not a stalker. And yes, it's Geoff." His hands lower, the corner of his mouth curving up in an adorable half-smile. "I swear I'm not following you. I stopped for coffee and bumped into Alessandra. She and I chatted a bit and she mentioned your name. She also mentioned you volunteered here."

Damn Lessa and her big mouth. She would tell anyone anything if they buttered her up first. I had to admit, though, seeing Geoff again did crazy things to my insides. Our brief encounter last night had thrown me off balance. Sleep almost non-existent. I came to the center today only to distract myself from my wayward thoughts.

Now that I was in his presence again, away from the darkness and energy of the club, I could get a better read on him.

Standing with his feet hip-width apart, he tucks his thumbs in his front pockets. He watches as I study his face, his eyes as still as the sea on a beautiful day. His lips curve up at the corners, the minute smile almost undetectable. But most of all, his demeanor calms me. I can't quite explain it, but him standing mere feet from me settles every adverse feeling I have known.

Last night shouldn't repeat itself. I didn't want to walk away from him again.

Something about him consumes every fiber inside me. Butterflies flap with vengeance in my belly, his smile affecting me like no other.

"That sounds like Lessa. And as much as I'd like to stand here and talk with you, I've had a rough day and need to go home and wind down."

Even as I say the words, I know I'm speaking partial truths. More than anything, I want to stand in front of him, talk for hours, and get lost at sea in his eyes. I lock onto his stunning blues for a breath before breaking contact. My thumb swipes over my key fob, not willing to press it yet.

Seconds stretch out our silence, his gaze heating every inch of me. Anxiety and foolishness lurk in my chest. Ready to escape the embarrassment, I bounce from foot to foot when he grazes my forearm.

I freeze.

God, it has been a long time since anyone touched me.

I close my eyes and sigh. Intimacy is something I have missed for years. His touch leaves a tingle along my skin. A warmth in my bloodstream. An ache in my chest for more.

He leans into my body, his lips a breath from my ear. "Magdalena, will you have dinner with me tonight?" His soft-spoken question adds a new layer to the buzz coursing throughout my body.

A simple question should provoke a simple answer. But dinner with Geoff would be anything except simple. A date with this man would be much more. Words entwining with actions and emotions. The promise of something new and desirable.

Just be yourself.

"Yes, I'll have dinner with you."

"I can pick you up or we can meet at the restaurant." The tip of his thumb rubs a small circle on my skin, leaving fire in its wake. "Whichever you prefer."

"I'll meet you there," I mumble before I give myself time to reconsider.

He retrieves his cell phone from his back pocket, unlocks the screen, and taps a few times.

"Will you add your contact info?"

He rests his phone in my palm, a blank contact screen open, giving me the upper hand.

I hesitate a few seconds. But once my fingers tap the keyboard, he exhales and drops his shoulders. I mask my smile as heat blushes my cheeks.

Rotating the phone in my palm, I hand it back to him.

"Thank you." His smile shines brighter than the sun above us. "I'll text you the details. Is meeting at six okay? Will that give you enough time to relax and get ready?"

I glance down at my watch to check the time. Two-forty-two. A few hours should be enough time to clear my mind of the happenings of the day and prepare myself, mind and body, to go on a date.

"Six would be great."

With a smile on his rugged face, Geoff nods and walks off.

In three hours, I'm going on a date. Three hours.

As I get into my car and drive home, my biggest concern is what the heck do I wear?

CHAPTER 6

MAGDALENA

It was five-twenty and I was two swipes of mascara and a touch of lip gloss away from being ready. The butterflies fluttering in my stomach intensified with each passing second. And they kicked in the moment I got his text with the restaurant details.

The warm, fragrant bubble bath did its magic, relaxing me and calming my brain after the day's activities at work, both inside the center and in its parking lot. I managed to unwind a lot quicker than usual, staying in the lavender-scented bath, letting it ease my aching muscles. Once the water cooled, I stepped out of the tub and headed for my closet.

I stared at the contents of my closet for a solid twenty minutes, not touching anything, my mind a blank canvas. I was utterly clueless as to what I should wear. It was half tempting to message Lena, but I knew that conversation would be littered with a load of questions I wasn't ready to answer yet.

Eventually, I opted for a cream-colored halter dress with a

navy sash, pairing it with navy flats. Dressy, but casual. I finished my hair in no time before starting my makeup.

Now, a bundle of anticipation sits low in my belly as I get in my car and head for the restaurant.

The restaurant we're meeting at is outside of town, between Olympia and Tacoma. Veering onto the highway, I'm relieved at the lack of traffic. But my relief fizzles away within seconds as nervous energy takes its place. It's been years since I dated.

My eyes on the road, I catch glimpses of the robust evergreens that line the highway. From the small opening of the windows, hints of earth and pine and rain in the distance filter through the air. On occasion, there is a break in the tree line— neighborhoods and shopping centers occupying the space. Families walking through mall parking lots. Children playing with one another on quiet streets. Noticing these little pieces of Washington reminds me of why I love living here. The perfect blend of nature and city and life.

The GPS audio quiets the music in the car, announcing the mileage before my exit. The shortening distance adds a new layer of dampness to my skin. An uptick to my pulse.

Instances like now have me missing my mom more. I would give anything to hear her advice. To have her warm arms wrap around me and hold me close. To memorize her wisdom. Wisdom I had little opportunity to hear.

Dad did his best after she passed. But Mom was irreplaceable.

Lessa's words from last month ring in my head, and they warm me the same way Mom did.

Just be yourself.

I inhale deep, resolving to do just that. Be myself.

Exiting the highway, I wind through the city. Within

minutes, the GPS guides me into a parking lot. I drive to the front and spot Geoff standing near the valet. He's clad in a snug, black dress shirt—the top button undone—khaki dress slacks, and black dress shoes. Sharp.

"Konnichiwa. Welcome to Agedashi," the valet says as he steps aside, bowing at the waist, his hand gesturing me toward a walkway.

Hell, I am so underdressed. My arms wrap around my middle. Geoff steps closer, stopping on my right with his elbow jutting out, a silent request to loop my arm in his. I oblige.

We walk along the slate pathway to the restaurant, neither of us saying another word. But Geoff's eyes scorch my skin.

The exterior is decorated with an ornate Japanese rock garden, a ravine and pond stocked with koi. Unfamiliar bonsai plants and colorful flowers line the pond embankment. Plucked chords of music float in the air. Small lanterns span the walkway to light the path, enough to see our way when the sun drops below the horizon, setting an intimate tone.

As we reach the entrance to the restaurant, Geoff turns to me. "You look beautiful tonight. Your dress is lovely." A glint sparks in his eyes and the butterflies from earlier flutter with ferocity.

Even in the dimming daylight, I'm confident he can see the blush on my cheeks. If not, the slight rise in my body temperature would be noticeable with our still-connected arms. He gives nothing away, though, and proceeds to the doors that open as we approach.

The maître d' verifies our reservation then leads us to a table down a small corridor. We pass a section of lush bamboo that blocks the diners from the entryway.

The corridor ends, displaying the dining area, each table

shrouded in privacy. The lighting throughout the restaurant low, candles the focal point. We're guided to an outdoor terrace where a teak table sits under a jasmine-covered pergola. Small lights twinkle between the vines, adding soft elegance and highlighting a koi pond. A small cluster of candles sit in the center of the table, the setting more romantic than I expected tonight.

Geoff sits beside me, satisfaction brightening his expression with the location of our table. Until now, I hadn't realized we were the only table on the terrace. We would have complete privacy throughout the evening.

He turns toward me, a shy smile set in place, or perhaps it's a nervous smile. I didn't know the difference in his smiles. Yet. Maybe it was all in my head. He carried himself with subtle confidence on the two occasions I had seen him thus far.

Should I start looking through the menu? Should I start some chitchat?

Dating is so foreign to me. The last guy I dated was five years ago. Three months into the relationship, my dad had a stroke. And the guy stopped calling. The few dates I have been on were never in as secluded a setting either. My knee bounces below the table. I swipe up the menu and scan the laminated pages, not absorbing any of it.

Starting conversations has never been my strong suit. Do I just blurt out random things? Do I ask him how his day was? It all seems so odd to me.

The sudden warmth of Geoff's hand on my knee halts me. My eyes flick to his.

"Calm down, Magdalena. There's no reason to be so nervous. Tonight is about getting to know one another. I don't have any expectations, and I would never do anything to make you uncomfortable. Alright?"

Calm washes over me. His touch is a balm, his voice a sweet caress. Undiluted tranquility wiping away my anxiety and replacing it with solace.

"Alright. Sorry about that, it's been a long time since I've dated and I'm a little lost."

He smiles at me with tenderness and I can't help but reciprocate. We return to our menus as a middle-aged woman dressed in an intricate, floor-length Japanese robe walks out to greet us.

"Good evening, sir, miss. Do either of you have any questions?"

We look at each other, then back to the waitress, shaking our heads.

We order drinks and the waitress scurries off, giving us a minute to read the menu.

The vast menu overwhelms me and I slip into a stupor, lost in the countless options. Geoff's hand gives me a light squeeze and I reply with a shy smile.

"Have you decided on what to eat?"

"Honestly, I don't know much about Japanese food beyond the places that cook on the table. So, I'm stumped on where to even begin."

A lightness dances across his face. It's subtle but noticeable. "Do you trust me? If I choose for us, is that okay?"

By some strange twist of cosmic fate, I do trust him. "Yes," I whisper.

A radiant smile lights his face.

I clear my throat, praying our drinks arrive soon. "What are we having?"

His eyes return to the menu and the loss of contact saddens me. "Sukiyaki with wagyu beef. A friend raved about it. It should be a fun experience since we cook it ourselves. Sorry, no onion volcanos that turn into trains here." He chuckles, his lower lip jutting out in a mock pout. And it's adorable.

The waitress returns with our drinks—*thank god*. Geoff orders for us, the waitress vanishing seconds later.

I gaze up at the twinkling pergola, breathing in the appealing perfume and take in the scenery encompassing us. A most magnificent ambiance. So calming and soothing and romantic.

For a moment, I close my eyes, allowing my senses to absorb it all. The soft fragrance of the jasmine, the trickle of the water falling into the pond, the night summer air on my skin, the warmth radiating off the fascinating man at my side. It's almost like an escape to another world, familiar and not at the same time.

"What are you thinking about?" His whisper adds another layer to my heightened senses.

My eyes open, slow and measured, and take him in.

His crystalline blues smolder and I fidget in my seat.

"It's difficult to translate. I'm just absorbing everything. This place. You. How it all makes me feel." I swallow. "More than once tonight, I've been anxious about our date. Wondering how it would go. I haven't dated in a while. And somehow, you manage to help me overcome my anxiety each time it surfaces and I'm bewildered by that. I've never been so at ease, yet ignited. Just being near you... it's peaceful. And energizing. I don't think I'm explaining myself quite right, but I like the way it feels."

Now when his brilliant blue eyes bore into mine, I return the gaze without hesitation. A new version of bravery coursing throughout my body. But after a moment of silence passes, I question my bravery.

Did I say too much?

"So, it's not just me that feels this... tug?" he asks. "I know we know next to nothing about each other. But I want to know you, Magdalena. Every part of you. And not just the smiles and laughs, but also the tears and sadness. I hope I'm not being too forward."

Too forward? I just word vomited my emotions to this man and he was asking me if he was *too forward*?

"No, not too forward," I mutter. As strange as that may sound coming from either of us right now.

As much as I want to know everything about Geoff, I don't want to interject that into this moment. I want, and don't want, small talk. Small talk devalues a genuine conversation, in my mind. So I opt for bravery in place of small talk. I slide my hand down, resting it over his. Something surges through me at the touch. I'm alive, in a pure and new way.

With just a touch or whispered word from him, my world is more even keeled. My soul unearthing a new solace.

Moments pass and we sit here, neither of us moving, neither of us speaking a word. His weight shifts, ever so slightly, as he leans into me. The movement is interrupted when the waitress appears with our food. We both pull away, making an effort to focus on her for the moment, although the heat coursing through me makes focusing tricky.

The waitress gives us a small, practiced smile. "Sukiyaki is a traditional dish that cooks at the table. I will start everything and explain as we go, then you can add items when you want to cook them. The vegetables need more time than the beef."

A giant, somewhat flat, circular pot is set on the table, a small propane burner underneath. She adds vegetable broth and a sauce and allows it to heat up. Next, she adds various vegetables and thick, clear noodles, stirring everything with chopsticks.

The whole process is fascinating, and I cannot wait to eat. The waitress cracks two eggs into individual bowls, scrambling them, and setting them before us.

"Now we cook the beef. Just place the piece into the pot and cook it a minute or two. Then, you'll dip the beef in the egg and eat."

Uh… I don't remember hearing anything about a raw egg.

My deer in the headlights expression must give me away, because the waitress rushes to reassure me.

"When you dip the hot meat in the egg, the heat cooks the thin coating of egg."

I exhale and relax into my seat more. "Oh...of course. Thank you."

My next thought… *Where's my fork?* Because all I see is chopsticks and I haven't practiced enough to be proficient. As if reading my mind, Geoff speaks up before I can ask the waitress for cutlery.

"You don't need a fork. Allow me to help you with the first bite, and then I'll show you how to use your chopsticks."

I give him a doubtful look, but he just smiles in response and the waitress leaves us to our meal.

Geoff takes a slice of the egg-dipped beef and brings it to my lips, my mouth parting slowly. His mouth curves into one of the sexiest grins I have ever seen, and I would cave to any of his requests in this moment. The meat hits my tongue, the savory beef melting. My lips hold the chopsticks captive as a faint moan rumbles in my chest. And he returns the sentiment.

Heat scatters throughout my body. My breath and pulse erratic. Between the man, the setting, and the food—it's over-stimulating.

I'm so enraptured by him in this moment, and I have a newfound desire to experience everything with him.

"Would you like me to show you how to use your chopsticks now?" Geoff offers.

He still wears his intoxicating grin, the one that makes me want to forego eating. I shake my head, knowing there is no way I'd grasp the lesson offered. Not tonight, anyway. He slides away from me to leave the booth.

"I'll get you a fork. Hang on a moment."

Before he can make it far, I capture his hand in mine. "No, you misunderstand me. You can show me, but I don't think I'll figure it out before the food gets cold." I gaze at my hand on his before I return my focus to his. "You may need to spot me while I eat," I giggle.

He chuckles, his head shaking subtly. He wasn't laughing at me, but perhaps at my asking him to assist me.

"Perhaps we can save the lesson for next time. What do you think of the food? Different than you expected?"

I nod. I watch his hand, longing for more as the chopsticks reach his lips. More food. More words. More intimacy. More of anything he has to offer.

For the first time in my life, all I want is more.

CHAPTER 7

GEOFFREY

By far, Magdalena has proven to be the most glorious distraction.

Clasping the chopsticks firmly between my fingers, I add more meat to the pot cooking our dinner. Prepared to continue feeding us both, I study her features. Her brows knit together, a deep concentration on display, consuming me with the desire to know what is going through that beautiful mind of hers.

Coordinating the chopsticks, I remove a slice of the meat from the pot, ready to dip it in the egg bowl when she closes her eyes. Is she having second thoughts about everything?

But my concern slips away the second I hear what follows.

A raspy moan spills from her chest and it's like nothing I have ever heard.

At the sound, my chopstick-laden hand freezes above the pot, a thin piece of beef trapped between the two wooden utensils. I gape at her, hesitant.

Magdalena surfaces emotions I buried long ago. Feelings I

swore off after Charlotte. Heartbreak I'm not willing to experience again.

Shaking off the past, I focus on the woman in front of me.

Is she turned on by this?

The thought does nothing to curtail my desire. My attraction to Magdalena is undeniable. Every molecule in my body calls out to her as if I have known her for years.

Reality slaps me the moment I realize she is more than a distraction. From the second I laid eyes on her—the way my body stirred back to life—it should have been clear as day she'd always be more than just a distraction.

I sip my water and push past my revelation.

Rotating toward her, I deliver the waiting food. Her lips part, her mouth asking for what only I can bestow upon it.

The food hits her tongue, her lips tightening together around the chopsticks, stopping their retreat briefly before she frees them. Am I a pervert for enjoying the way her lips wrap around the chopsticks? For loving the groan of pleasure that follows? For staring at her lips without shame? A surge of heat spikes throughout my body and thunders in my groin.

Time ticks by, the silence stretching between us, the thrumming of my pulse all I hear. My fingertips graze the soft skin on her forearm from elbow to wrist. A current pulses in my veins at the contact.

Can she sense it too?

I lean into her, my lips at her ear, and breathe her in. A hint of vanilla and rose. It's heady, being this close. We sit a hair's breadth apart for several breaths.

My voice is a whisper unrecognizable to my own ears. "Magdalena, your beauty does crazy things to me. I'm doing everything within my power to remain a gentleman, but I'm not sure if I can resist you much longer."

Against my own will, I back away. Just enough to see the entirety of her face in front of mine, her eyes closed. I study the length of her lashes and how they meet the small patch of freckles below her eyes. She doesn't move, doesn't say a word.

Waiting for a response turns nerve-wracking. She doesn't flinch. Doesn't give anything away.

Finally, the softest of sighs leaves her lips, her body leaning into me. The sudden rush is exhilarating and overwhelming all at once. She is so close, yet not close enough. And it sets my soul on fire.

The warm tenderness of her lips makes contact with mine, and I pause, absorbing the wave of heat striking my chest. Her lips brush over mine without hurry, covering me in small, feathery kisses. Reading my lips as if they're braille and hers were fingertips. The energy passing from her into me...

More. I want more.

The warmth of her breath skims along my jaw, her lips grazing along the edge of my chin. A newfound thrill spreads over every inch of my skin and fuses at my groin. She is going to unman me in this restaurant. I'm not sure I could stop her. I'm not sure I want to stop her.

When her lips find mine again, I test her boundaries, my tongue slipping past her lips and tasting her for the first time. Sweet and delicious, like a vanilla-sin swirl. The taste drives me wild, makes me ravenous. Has me craving to taste more.

The intensity of the kiss ratchets up with each stroke of our tongues, my need for her amplifying with each passing beat. She's sucking on my tongue now, devouring me as if her life depended on it.

Devour is not a strong enough word for what my body wants to do to hers. I return her fervor, pulling away from her mouth and tracing her jawline, suckling along the lines of her neck and tasting the delicate skin along her clavicle.

The combination of her scent and taste hits me all at once, driving me over the edge. Especially because I'm unable to do anything to remedy the situation right now. Somehow, I force myself back from her.

And her eyes pop open. Hazel wrapped in brilliant green, fogged with pleasure.

"Why did you stop?" she asks.

I catch my breath and reply, "I stopped because we're still at the restaurant. Someone could walk back any minute. And I'd prefer no one sees us making out at the table. Also, anything else we may, or may not do, should be somewhere more comfortable and private. Okay?"

Not five seconds later, the waitress returns to the table. A sweet smile perks up her timeless face when she notices our proximity. A rosy hue paints her cheeks before she offers to package our remaining food. Setting everything on a cart, she wheels the food away, promising to return with our check.

"I have a confession," I whisper. "Tonight is the first time I've been so... overtaken by a woman." I can't place it, but something about Magdalena compels me to open myself to her. "Lust is usually all I allow myself to feel. Most women serve only as a distraction. Honestly... That was what I thought you might be. A great distraction." I wipe my palms up and down my thighs. "But in the short time we've known each other, this" —I gesture between us— "feels different."

Magdalena remains silent, her stillness shooting my anxiety up a notch. Was my confession too much? Perhaps she is replaying it in her head to formulate a response. Most women blurt out the first thing they think of. But Magdalena isn't like most women.

She absorbs everything and then speaks her resolve. She prefers clear, decisive outcomes. It is a refreshing quality I haven't seen in years. And she continues to amaze me at each turn.

Understanding skitters across her features. "Thank you. Thank you for being honest. The few dates I've been on weren't like this. Or you. I'll confess, a relationship isn't at the top of my To-Do list either. And I've never made out in public before. Ever." Her cheeks flush a beguiling pink. "But with you… everything is different, better. New and scary and invigorating."

Her unexpected confession has me contemplative. Should I ask her? What if she says no? Or… What if I never ask and she would've said yes?

"This might be out of line, but…" I pause, holding my breath until I can say the words. "Would you like to continue what we started?"

She ponders over my words, but not as long as I thought she would. "Yes. I just don't want to make any promises."

I nod. "Magdalena, I have no expectations of how the evening will be. Okay?"

Before she can respond, the waitress returns with our food and hands me the bill. I slap my card on top and hand it back. The waitress startles, but takes it and scurries off.

"Someone's in a hurry to leave," Magdalena says with a hint of muffled laughter.

"Maybe just a little." I pinch my thumb and forefinger close together. "Can you blame me? I'm sitting next to the most beautiful woman I've ever set eyes on. The kicker? She wants to leave as much as I do, I think, and continue our little make-out session."

While pointing out the obvious, I keep things light and

humorous. She leans closer to me, her breath hitching. And her reaction has my heart racing. Although she doesn't come right out and say it, she hints enough to let me know.

My compliment sends a new rush of scarlet to her cheeks, accentuating her freckles. Is she embarrassed by what I said? Or is she uncomfortable with my flattery? Perhaps she's as turned on by our kiss as I am.

I sign the credit card slip, the waitress thanking us before walking away. The moment she's out of sight, I'm eager for us to leave. Stepping out of the booth, I grab the food and offer my hand to Magdalena. She places her hand in mine with zero hesitation and slides out of the booth.

Her hand in mine is perfect. How it should be.

Unlike our walk into the restaurant, when we took our time to check out the setting, we are now rushing toward the exit. It may be unnoticeable to onlookers, but we're both aware, and I whisper-laugh.

"What are you laughing at?" she asks, lines crinkling her forehead.

"I'm laughing at our hasty departure."

Her sweet giggle flicks a spark in my chest and I smile. It's a musical sound. One I hope to never forget.

We reach the valet, our cars awaiting us, the maître d' informing the valet upon our departure. I tip the valet, and he walks back to his podium.

"Let's meet at my place," Magdalena suggests.

"If you're comfortable with that, I am. I don't want to pressure you into anything."

She nods. "Let me give you my address, in case we get separated."

I hand her my phone after pulling up her contact profile. My eyes follow her fingers as she taps the screen. Earlier today,

I would never have suspected my day to end like this. With me following Magdalena—a mysterious woman I couldn't get out of my head—to her home after our date.

A moment later, we drive off and head for her house.

The drive back to Lake Lavender flies by and I've had no time to process what's about to happen. In half the time it took to get to the restaurant, I'm now parking behind Magdalena's car in her driveway. And she invited me here. It's all so surreal.

I cut the engine and amble to her car. When she peers up at me, the energy between us shifts. Clouds of nervousness and excitement hover between us. A little nervousness is okay, but only the good kind. Does she still want me to stay?

"Magdalena, me coming inside your house is your choice. Don't feel pressured or obligated, especially from me. This is your decision to make, but I need your certainty."

She wrestles her fingers at her waist, her hazel eyes soft and packed with emotion. Will she oblige? Or will she reject the idea, now that we're here? *Patience. Just have patience.*

"You say it's my choice, but I don't agree. I'll admit, the gesture is appreciated, but you and I both know the decision was made long before now. Mine was made when you stopped me at Black Silk. And if I had to guess, yours was made before that, when I saw you watching me."

I'm struck dumb, something that doesn't often occur, but she is spot on with her assessment. The moment my eyes landed on her, I had to know her. As if some cosmic force directed me straight to her.

What can I say?

There's nothing to say. So, I nod as she leads us to her front door.

We step inside, a lamp flickering on as she sets her clutch and keys on the foyer table.

"Would you like a drink?"

She takes the food packages from my hand and heads toward the kitchen. I follow quietly in her wake.

In the kitchen, she stands in front of the fridge, her back to me. I step close. Close enough to brush her skin with the edges of my shirt. Her body freezes as if she's aware I'm an inch from touching her. Her breath hitches and the sound sends my heart into a frenzy.

I step closer and lean down, grazing her ear with my lips.

"I don't want a drink." My breath hot on her neck, lust rasping my voice. "What I do want is to peel this dress off of you. To run my fingers over your soft skin and feel every part of you tremble beneath my touch along the way. I want to taste every part of you."

She closes the fridge, her chest rising and falling in quick bursts, her hands dropping to her sides. She stands there, waiting for further direction. Waiting for my lips and hands to dance across her skin.

How should I approach this? After all, we did just have half of a first date. But didn't her behavior match mine? All obvious cues lead to yes. Still, I can't assume my own desires mimic hers.

Tipping my head forward, I drop a cascade of soft kisses along her shoulder. She shudders, her temperature rising against my lips. She doesn't say a word. Doesn't move a muscle. But her breathing encourages me onward. My body moves of its own volition, my hand finding the curve of her hip, my thumb caressing circles while my fingers squeeze the soft surface under her dress.

My lips break away from her skin a moment, peppering kisses between my words as I speak. "I could stay in this kitchen with you all night and do countless things on various surfaces, but I'd much rather go somewhere more comfortable."

I've thrown the ball in her court since she still hasn't said yes. My hands continue caressing her hip, my lips savoring her shoulder and neck while I wait. Praying she acquiesces. Hunger builds inside me as she tips her head to the side more, granting me full access to her neck.

A slow turn of her head and she's pinning me in place, her heated eyes piercing my erratic heart. "Follow me."

Two words. They fulfill all I ask and much more. She laces my fingers in hers and guides us out of the kitchen and down a hallway. The house is larger than I'd suspected.

We walk past two doors, one on each side of the hall, before reaching a third. She stops, inhaling before turning to face me. I study her expression, my eyes darting between hers. *Is she having second thoughts?*

Her quiet voice pierces the dark, silent hall. "Geoff, it's been a long time since I've been with anyone. On a date or intimately. I just wanted you to know. Not out of pity, but in case I act *off*. I can't ignore what's happening between us, but it intimidates me."

I lean into her, taking her mouth with mine. My tongue sweeps over hers, her soft moan vibrating against my lips. It delivers a jolt straight to my cock, and the only word in my head is *more*—flashing like a neon sign.

Holy fuck.

Her arm moves behind her and the door handle clicks. Her weight shifts and her feet step backward, leading us in the room. The second we pass the threshold, a frantic hunger flits throughout my body. I want more. I *need* more.

My hands skim away from her hips, sliding up the sides of her torso and tracing around to her backside. My fingers brush the clasp of her halter dress at the base of her neck, releasing the hooks.

She inhales deep, then exhales as she grabs ahold of my shirt, the fabric bunching in her palms. I drop one hand from her neck, descending to the zipper at her waist, fondling her creamy, soft skin along the way.

Reaching the fastener, I lay my palm flat against her back. Desire ripples off her in waves, her mouth feeding mine. Her hands dance along the front of my shirt and stroke my chest beneath the fabric. She drops a hand to rest over mine, the hand on her lower back, her unspoken request encouraging me to continue undressing her.

Waiting for me to slide the zipper down the teeth, her drive intensifies. Her desire is a living, breathing entity—its essence filling the room, pulsating around us. Making me insatiable. Driving me further. And I'm no longer able to resist, the potency of her too powerful to deny either of us.

The fastener in my fingertips, I slide my hand down and part the teeth of the zipper. As the fabric puddles at her feet, her body goes rigid beneath my touch.

CHAPTER 8

MAGDALENA

My nerves are on fire, but my body is frozen.

I clutch his shirt tight, but he angles away from me. "Are you okay?"

My need for him wipes away every rational thought and I nod. Clenching my fists, I tug on his shirt, the threads complaining under my force.

An electrical current buzzes under his touch along the edge of my panties, then traces up the curve of my backbone. A shiver rolls up my spine when his fingers dance along the base of my neck.

Soft, delicate strokes skim my biceps. His fingers trickle down my forearms, taking my hands and removing them from his shirt.

His unhurried tempo drives my hunger for him, edging me closer with each breath and touch that grazes my skin. My hands fidget in his as I try to break free.

Stepping out of the dress, I walk us backward. The coolness of the comforter a juxtaposition to my heated skin as it brushes the back of my knees. Dizziness reigns over my body.

I break our kiss, my lungs burning. Tipping my head back, I gasp, "Oh god." Because it all feels so good. Blissfully good. His lips trail my cheekbone, leaving light kisses tattooed onto my skin.

Musk and teakwood and pure masculinity invade my nose. His lips graze my earlobe before his teeth clamp down. Lips and tongue roam and caress and memorize the exposed flesh along my neck and shoulders. And I'm in sensation overload, my skin fevered, my blood molten. He is everywhere—surrounding and taking over my body.

Arousal surges, rising up my throat and spilling out my lips, the carnal sounds intense and heady.

Hot air blankets the skin below my ear. His hands release me, framing the sides of my face and pulling me into him, devouring me.

My hands itch to remove his shirt. I trace down the buttoned hemline, brushing along the waistline of his pants. I tease his abdominals, his muscles contracting under the cotton. With deft hands, I tug at the ends of his shirt and expose his flesh.

My knuckles brush along the brim of his pants, stroking my discovered treasure. His abdomen dips under my touch as he hisses through his teeth. He rewards me with kisses along the line of my collarbone. Then he pauses at the base of my throat, jolting me when his hands skim the sides of my breasts.

His mouth kisses lower. Warm, delicate fingers map the contours of my breasts. And the buzz coursing inside me is like nothing I have encountered before. My lace panties and the darkness are the only things shielding my modesty. With his clothes still intact, I'm suddenly self-conscious.

My arm flies up and covers my breasts. He rises and

presses against my body, searching my eyes. "Did I do something wrong?"

But I stand, speechless, again. All I can do is shake my head. My face heats with embarrassment. He didn't do anything wrong. In fact, he was doing so many things right. But how can I tell him I'm only a few sexual encounters short of virginity?

He caresses the arm shielding my breasts. "You don't need to hide from me, Magdalena. You are beautiful. Stunning." His lips kiss my skin between his words. "Clothes or not. Please don't feel ashamed. Please. Not with me. I want to know you. All of you."

His thumb brushes across my cheek, eliciting a new trail of sparks. His lips press a gentle kiss to mine. He traces small circles on my hipbone with his thumb. And slowly, my embarrassment fades. He has given me the greatest gift of all.

Courage.

He leans forward, kissing me with such tenderness. I lower my arms, lacing my fingers in his belt loops and dragging him closer, our bodies back in sync.

Seconds after, goose pimples spread over my skin as he steps back from me, his eyes tracing the lines of my frame. The attention has mortification rearing its ugly head, but I swallow it down.

"Gorgeous," he whispers.

His compliment sucks the air from my lungs. It's strange, hearing admiration from someone who barely knows me. The impact strikes harder for it. What do I say? Do I thank him? But before I can form a cohesive thought, he continues.

"I want to memorize every freckle, every scar, every dip and curve of your body. I want to navigate every inch. Learn what makes your pulse soar and your breath ragged. Know where your mind goes when I have my mouth on your skin. Hear your cries and moans as I lick your curves and move inside you."

Holy fuck. I have never given dirty talk any merit, but holy hell.

Even inches away, his voice is breathy and labored. His arms hang at his sides, his stance open. Mouth slack, his tongue wets his lower lip, then he bites the flesh between his teeth and holds it briefly before it pops out, the visible moisture making me hungry to taste him again.

"Yes. *Please.*" The simple plea rolls off my tongue. Desire consumes me, my body trembling with the promise of what is yet to come.

His voyeurism alters my apprehension, my previous desire to hide slipping away. An awareness in me shifts, and I become this new, wanton creature. Someone I never knew existed. The urge to be flesh to flesh with him is undeniable.

My nimble fingers unbutton his shirt, a flutter in my stomach erupts as each comes undone. My eyes follow the path of my fingers, watching as each button unfastens, the anticipation of what will happen next heightening every nerve ending in my body.

I reach the final button, his shirt still closed. Inhaling deep, I run both hands up the center of his chest, slipping them under the parted fabric. Spreading it apart, I slide it off his shoulders and watch it fall to the floor.

My hands travel over the newly exposed ridges and planes of his chest. My fingers tell me what my eyes cannot in the dim, moonlit room. Trailing the length of his collarbones, his shoulders rise and fall under my fingertips, my palms pressing to his chest, stroking the musculature of his pecs. I slide my hands down, the soft ripples along his abdomen defined, contracting under my touch. His bobbing Adam's apple distracts me, halting my hands.

His fingers clutch my chin, lifting and tipping my head back to bring my eyes to his. His mouth drops to mine like gravity plummeting to the earth. His lips are deliberate as a low groan vibrates in his chest. Sparks ignite as his hands trek the length of my body, settling when his thumbs tuck under my lace panties. His lips sweep across my cheek, his breath heavy as he whispers.

"When you look at me, when your hands touch my skin, it's beyond arousing. And when you kiss me... There's an animal, deep within my core clawing its way out, begging me to consume you."

Pressing his chest against mine, my breasts melding to his upper abdominals, he lowers us onto the bed. His lips are at my ear, nipping the lobe between his teeth, trailing kisses down my neck and along my clavicle.

His hands knead along the sides of my body, slow at first. Returning just below my arms with a firm grip, he slides me up the bed farther. The bed dips, giving way to the added weight now above me. His bewitching, blue eyes bore into mine, a quick intake before he lowers himself, stealing my breath once more. This kiss is different. More passionate. Every thread of his desire flowing into me.

My hands dance over his muscular back, running the length of his spine a few times, memorizing them as they contort and contract. Our fervor multiplies, stirring an ache in me, a new and possessive sensation. As my fingers reach the edge of his pants, ready to return on their path back north, I sink my nails into his lower back.

A harsh growl bleeds into our kiss, his hands cupping my face, holding me in place as our tongues continue their escapade. In a deliberate, measured move, I scrape my nails along the sidelines of his spine, up to his neck, his back arching into my touch, our lips never parting. Our kiss deepens and is unrelenting. His body adjusts, the weight of him more prevalent as he presses the length of his arousal between the junction of my thighs.

I slide one hand down his back, slipping my fingertips under the edge of his pants, tracing it around to his front. For a moment, I tease the small trail of hair at his waistline and then shift my hips so I can slide my hand between us, wanting the weight of him in my palm.

The soft heat is an unexpected contrast to the firm stone laid beneath it. He throws his head back, thrusting himself into my palm furthermore.

"God, that feels so good," he groans, low and deep. And the ache between my legs turns fiery.

The endless teasing could be the death of me. But I'm not sure I am ready for sex yet.

My fingers seize the button at the front of his pants, unfastening it and sliding the zipper to its endpoint. Slipping my hands under the fabric, I shove his pants down his legs.

We were equals now, his form-fitting boxer briefs and my scant lace panties the only barrier between us. Pressure grinds against my lace-covered mound, his length rubbing the swollen bundle of nerves at my apex. My back bows off the bed, my breasts crushing into his chest as I whimper. Pure agonizing bliss.

His lips trail down my neck, my nails composing new lines on his back. Shifting his weight, his lips trace the outer edge of my breast. Fingers grasping my flesh with severity, his breath spiking with my own. His lips move inward, sucking and nibbling until they land on the pert bud.

"Argh," I cry out.

His mouth wraps around the peak, the reverberation spilling from his body erotic and unhinged. A hand takes hold of my other breast, kneading the fleshy mound, his mouth switching sides and taking the neglected bud.

My hips buck, grinding along the ridge of his arousal, my hands clutching both cheeks of his ass, drawing him further into my desire. My breath hitches, my body screaming for his, the urge to have him inside me building.

His tongue sweeps to the base of my throat, licking between my breasts, down my abdomen and halts above my panties. He veers toward my left hipbone, nipping and licking, his hands kneading my breasts.

Slower than I'd prefer, he inches to my right hip, embellishing it equal measure. His hands drift down my sides, edging to my hips and under my ass, lifting me. His eyes peek up to mine, dilated with greed and desire, one last request of reassurance. I rock my hips up.

A wicked, sexy grin spreads across his face, his nose coursing from my belly button down to the top of the lace, his lips at the top of my mound.

Motionless, his eyes close, his breath growing hotter. Like an addicted voyeur, I stare at him, the unknown turning me on more than imaginable. Taking a deep breath and holding it a few seconds, he opens his mouth, his jaw cupping my sex. No teeth, no tongue, just heat. And then he grinds his jaw against my clit, the sensation intense, driving my desire to push into him for more.

His eyes open, their slow gaze meeting mine, the intensity in them searing me. A straight shock to my core. A guttural moan builds in his chest, vibrating up his throat and into his mouth, eliciting an infinite ache between my legs. His hands slide to the front of my hips, kneading, but all I see is a set of crystalline blue eyes, begging for more. His fast fingers pry at my panties, tugging them away, his hot tongue tasting my bare apex.

"You're so sweet on my tongue. Tasting you every day... it would never be enough."

I throw my head back and give myself over to everything he is delivering. His tongue lavishes me with such precision. It's as if he is everywhere. It's all-consuming and my legs quiver in ecstasy, bliss seizing me. My body escalates to unfamiliar heights, the heat and intensity overwhelming. My lungs sucking in short, pitched breaths. His mouth more vigilant, his tongue more vigorous, my body meeting its pinnacle and discovering a euphoria I have never known.

No one has ever done that to me. Driven me to the precipice and sent me over the edge. The world spins a dizzy circle around me.

Just when I thought I could never feel anything more intense, he pushes his tongue deep into my core. The sensation adds fuel to the fire, my euphoria in a perpetual cycle. My body trembling, my arms and legs jelly. My breath ragged, the pitch in my moan escalating, no end in sight.

And then... I am gone. Shattered.

My vision blurs and I close my eyes. My orgasm pours out of me onto his quick tongue until every ounce of my being is satiated.

CHAPTER 9
GEOFFREY

S unlight pierces through my eyelids. The light flooding in is odd, penetrating every angle of the room. Confusion fills my every thought as my mind tries to figure out how the one small window in my bedroom could be letting in so much light. When I crack my lids, the glowing haze turns sharp.

This is not my bedroom.

With my head resting on a too soft pillow, my eyes land on large framed photographs of various flowers on the wall. The images beautiful and sad, the flowers residing in a darker background. As if they're alone in the shadows.

Where the hell am I? I bolt upright.

Like a slap in the face, reality strikes and I close my eyes. Images of last night flicker like a slideshow in my memory. Her rosy-vanilla scent wafting through the air and I inhale deep. The sting on my flesh a reminder of her animalistic side as she clawed along my spine. Her sweet, desperate cries as I brought her to orgasm with my tongue.

Magdalena.

I was in a powerful place with her last night. A place more potent than any other I'd experienced. I have zero recollection of being so enthralled with a woman before. And I am lost in everything her—her warmth, her smell, her soft, supple skin, the way her body reacts to my touch.

Lying next to her, after hours of indulging in one another, I must have fallen asleep. I have never been so exhausted in my life. God, I hope my presence, and potential unwanted overnight status, did not freak her out. Or cause her to wonder if she'd made a mistake. The mere thought makes my stomach tense.

Minutes tick by as I sit on her vintage floral pattern covered bed. Beyond the sliding glass door, Magdalena sits on a padded lounge chair on her porch, a throw blanket wrapping her snug. She sips on a mug of steamy liquid and stares out at the wilderness beyond a small patch of grass in her back yard. She did not move an inch, except when she would twirl a small piece of hair around her fingers, so deep in her own thoughts.

What is she thinking about? Is she thinking about me? About us? About what happened between us last night?

I don't want to disturb the apparent peace she's enjoying, but I also do want to disrupt her, to let her know I'm awake. To tell her that if she wants me to leave, I will. I'm sure she is just wrapping her mind around what happened last night, as I am.

My thoughts run on a continuous loop, a single idea repeating itself over and over—I need more of her. Not only more of her beauty, but also her words. Not only more of her body, but also her soul.

Some thoughts are difficult to translate into words, but all I know, deep down in my bones… She makes me feel alive.

It has been years since I've been *alive*. Years since I craved a woman for more than sex. Years since I wanted more. More than one night. More than one kiss.

Rising from the bed, I locate my clothes, putting them on but not buttoning my shirt and leaving my shoes off.

I tug open the door as quietly as I can. A soft pop sounds as the seal of the door separates.

A tender expression meets my eyes as she looks over at me, her cheeks creasing as she smiles. A smile that says she is happy to see me, but also that I am invading a private moment. I want to mimic her smile, but it seems off-putting.

"Morning. I didn't mean to interrupt you. You looked so peaceful sitting out here. I can go if you'd like."

Please don't tell me to leave.

"Hey, good morning. No, you're okay. Sitting out here every morning is just something in my normal routine of things. But I kind of space out and forget how long I'm out here." Her light chuckle at the end relaxes me a little, even with the monotone note in her voice.

I didn't want to make her feel any obligation to stop something she does every day, but I also didn't want to feel like I'm invading her space or time. "It's okay. I can head out if I'm throwing off your morning."

Please say that I'm not.

"You aren't throwing it off, exactly. It's just been a long time since I've woken up and had another person in my house. I need to wrap my mind around it a bit."

Her eyes are fixed on something in the distance, a sullen expression taking hold. My first thought is to ask her what has her sad. But since we've only known each other for no time at all, I opt to not ask such deep questions yet. Another time in the future, once we're more comfortable with each other.

But right now, I simply want more time with her, and

maybe this moment is not the time to have it. "Have you eaten anything yet? We can grab some breakfast if you'd like."

A different smile lights her face. It's sweeter. Almost endearing. A smile worth seeing again.

"Breakfast sounds nice. It'll take me a little time to get ready, if you'd like to go home and change. We can meet at nine at Java and Teas Me. They have an extensive menu on the weekends."

Her words are a statement, something added to today's To-Do list. Everything inside me screams to not leave. But as long as I get more time with her, it's worth agreeing. "Sure, I'll see you there at nine," I say, hoping she doesn't detect the lull in my voice.

I step back into the bedroom and yank the door shut, the somewhat formal tone of her invitation making me question everything. I button my shirt, leaving the top two undone.

Why is she still on the porch?

Chest tight, I slip my shoes on. I peek over at her, and she sits in the same position as minutes ago.

Does she regret last night?

Everything about redressing myself is robotic. A routine I've performed countless times, but has never been so mind-numbing.

Leaving her house is strange and wrong. This is the first time I have left a woman's house and *wanted* her to stop me.

What's worse? She does not walk me to the door. In fact, she remains seated on the lounger on her porch. Not once does she look my way. Within seconds, a thousand thoughts ping in my head.

Maybe she feels awkward about last night and doesn't want to bring it up. Perhaps she regrets inviting me back to her house. She did say it had been quite some time since she'd been on a date, intimacy not included in the equation, but I hope she wasn't appeasing me. That's a guilt I don't think I could handle. I would never, intentionally, pressure a woman.

With reluctance, I walk out of her bedroom and wander toward the front door. When I reach it, I stand there a moment before peering behind me. There's no sign of her, nor have I heard the sliding glass door open. Leaving like this is wrong on so many levels. There should be some form of interaction between us. Some form of *see you soon* from one or both of us.

But there is nothing. Nothing except silence and unease.

Her front door clicks shut behind me with a thud and I'm left wondering where we go from here. Because as it stands, I have no idea.

CHAPTER 10

MAGDALENA

I grasp the large, metal handle, heaving the heavy wood-framed door toward me, the image of a fancy latte painted on the glass. Stepping into Java and Teas Me, I spot Geoff amongst the bustling Saturday breakfast crowd at a table in the corner.

As I approach, he looks nervous, maybe even timid, like a boy who's scared to talk to the girl he's crushed on for months. It's an interesting visual, considering he was all confidence and eagerness and assurance last night. I'm not sure what to make of this change, of his altered presence.

"Hey, sorry I'm late. I'm a little pokey in the mornings." Giving him an apologetic smile, I slide into my seat across from him.

"You're good. I got here only a minute or so before you."

He fumbles with the napkin wrapped silverware. *Do I make him nervous?* "Have you eaten here before? The food is awesome."

His fidgeting dissipates a fraction, his response even-keeled. "Only once. My normal breakfast is coffee. Do you have a favorite here?"

I pause a moment, wondering how often he has been here. Maybe more than I assumed. I'm not sure why, but it strikes me in an odd, protective way. Like he's invading a space that I consider mine. The café does have several regulars—Lessa is a marketing fanatic and knows how to draw people in. But for a moment, I get this strange feeling that maybe Geoff knows more about me than he's letting on. Either that or I'm paranoid.

"I have several favorites, but I've probably ordered bagels or the eggs benny more than anything else. The hollandaise sauce is killer." My mouth waters at the prospect of eating.

A smile sweeps across his face as he scans the menu, pondering what he should order. Although, I think his smile reflects the name of my most ordered breakfast dish. It's an adorable smile, and I bookmark it as a favorite.

His eyes pop up as he sets the menu on the table. After a minute of menu staring, he opts for the eggs benny. I assumed that would happen. So, I choose the Breakfast of Champions, the breakfast that could feed the two of us easily. Whatever, I'm hungry.

His grin mirrors mine when I mention my increased appetite but then twists in confusion. "Meatless sausage? Did I order the totally wrong dinner for us last night?"

"No, I eat meat on occasion, but not often. I would've said something otherwise. Promise."

His relief is evident. "Good. I'd hate to think I fed you something you don't like or can't eat."

"Seriously, it's okay. Speaking of okay... are you? Okay? You seem nervous or worried or something."

He sits across from me, eyes locked on me, trying to read

what I'm not saying. It was far from uncomfortable, but he has an aura so wholly different than what he exuded yesterday. *Did I do something wrong last night?* I'm at a loss as to what I should be feeling.

Moments pass before his eyes drift to my lips, his Adam's apple bobbing. "I'm good. I woke up this morning and was a little disoriented, not remembering right away I fell asleep in your bed. Then, I saw you sitting on your porch and wondered the same thing… *is she okay? Did I do something wrong?"*

"Geoff, you did nothing wrong. In fact, you did many things that are beyond right. It's just that it's been a long time since I've had any sort of relationship. In any capacity. I'm used to my routines, one of which is sitting on my porch every morning. I didn't know if I should've stayed inside with you or do what I normally do. I've been a creature of habit for so long, it's difficult to be anything else."

I'm hopeful he understands where I am coming from. Minus the last few days, I've led the same monotonous life for years and it isn't so simple to just stop and do something different.

After my dad suffered a stroke while driving home, my life changed. Not only was I his daughter, but I was also his primary caregiver for two-and-a-half years. It was tough going from college student to nurse and housekeeper, aiding my ailing father, plus finishing my degree online. Though even if Mom had been alive at the time, I'm not sure it would've been much different.

Yes, I've done some things out of character in the last few days. I admit it. But I did them at my pace and for a brief time. I'd be lying if I said I didn't enjoy Geoff's company, but I'm also not ready to switch up my entire life after one evening with someone new.

How do I tell him everything that has molded my life without sounding like a pity case? Most of my adult life, I have managed to keep the sad stories of my past between me, Lessa, and Lena. It's not a common practice to divulge *all things Mags* to other people. Most people don't stick around long enough to hear them anyway.

Yet there are so many things I wish to tell this handsome man, who seems so worried about what just happened between us. But I can't seem to find my voice.

I'm thankful when the server reaches our table, breaking the growing silence.

We place our orders and the server rushes away. Seconds later, the same silence returns.

Geoff and I sit idle and study each other. His shoulders settle, his hands resting open on the table, his body visibly relaxing in front of me. While his body language says one thing, his eyes tell me a wholly different story.

Worry. Question. Doubt. Thousands of reactions skid across his spellbinding blues. But I'm not sure if those emotions are explicit to him alone or if he is wondering if I'm feeling them.

"Geoff..." I let my voice hang between us a moment while I stare down at the table. He doesn't say a word, but I know he's watching me fiddle with the coffee creamers on the table. After a minute, I glance up and confirm what I'd assumed. His eyes sear into me.

"Geoff, first I'd like to say that last night—the restaurant, the food, you, and back at my house afterward—was amazing. I haven't been on a date or out with anyone, other than Lessa and Lena, in a long time. I don't think I can put into words how wonderful it all was."

"But?" That one word floats heavy in the air.

"No buts. I want you to know I couldn't have imagined a better evening."

"I had a wonderful time with you, also. And I'm sorry if I've made things weird this morning. I just have this nagging feeling, as if I've done something wrong."

He scans my face, his eyes searching and pleading with me, as if he's pulling the answers directly from my thoughts. What could I tell him without putting my whole life on the table? I am not ready for that. I am not prepared to release my safety net.

"You haven't done anything wrong, I swear. There's just a lot in my past that keeps me from opening up to new people."

"But we just..." He is referring to our night of no-holds-barred intimacy. I can read it all over him. And even though we didn't go beyond oral sex, it was more intimate than any other experience.

I reach across the table and place my hand over his. "Yes, we did. And I loved every single moment. I want to explain myself, but you have to bear with me. It's not something I talk about with anyone."

His shoulders let go, releasing their last bit of tension, as he exhales. "I'll do my best. But I'll admit, with what I'm feeling, patience is foreign to me. I've never been so intrigued by someone. You've reeled me in and I'm on the hook till you decide to keep me or release me."

His words put the pressure of Jupiter's atmosphere on my chest. I do my best to disguise my increasing anxiety, but it's a challenge.

"Geoff, I like you. A lot. But... that's super intense. How can you put something so heavy on me? You haven't even given me the opportunity to say my piece yet."

His gorgeous blue eyes widen. And I stare at him, dumbstruck. How do I decipher my feelings for him? I'm itching to share the deepest and darkest moments of my life with him, but am I ready for that? Am I ready to take a sledgehammer to the wall protecting my heart?

Can I let him in? Maybe. Does the idea scare the hell out of me? Without question.

"Magdalena." My name lingers between us, his thoughts obviously warring in his head. "What I'm feeling right now, it's all new to me." His brows twist for a split second.

"You can call me Mags, you know. Magdalena sounds so formal." We share a quick smile, the air between us lighter. I prop my elbows on the table and lean forward, my eyes holding his. Although we barely know each other, he'll never be an acquaintance. He'll always be more.

"Mags. I'm trying not to overwhelm you. Hell, I'm trying not to overwhelm myself right now."

Out of nowhere, the waitress arrives at our table with our breakfast. The sight and smell of pure heaven invades my senses, and I cannot wait to devour every morsel before me. It's a ton of food, but I'm not intimidated by it for a second. Geoff's hearty laugh fills the air as he watches me stalk my prey.

"You laugh at me now, but you just wait. The moment that eggs benny hits your tongue, you'll wish you had restraint."

I watch as he carefully cuts up his breakfast, making it all into bite-size pieces before he even puts a bite in his mouth. Me, on the other hand... I am massacring my breakfast as if the apocalypse is knocking at the door and this is my last meal.

"Are you always so delicate with your food?" I tease. As if we're in some sort of role reversal, he is acting the part of the proper lady and me the slovenly guy. I can't help but giggle at the irony.

"Do you always eat your food like you never learned how to use utensils? I mean seriously, the food won't run away."

His laugh hits me and I cannot help but return it, desperate to keep myself from spewing my breakfast at him. "Sorry. Not feeling very lady-like today."

The laughter between us seems unending.

But when his eyes widen after he tastes his breakfast, it's inevitable he is hooked. "I told you it was good."

Laughter echoes across the table as we continue eating with abandon. On occasion, I catch him watching me eat. I would flash him a small smile, letting him know I'd caught him. As the food disappears from our plates, I contemplate what to say next. I'm eager to share a part of myself with him, but not sure what. I suppose I could start with something generic and see where it goes.

"Amazing, wasn't it?"

"Every. Single. Bite."

"Knew it. That's why it's always a favorite," I say, nudging an orange peel around my plate with my fork.

The waitress leaves the bill at the table and removes our plates. I offer to pay, but Geoff turns down the notion. After he slips cash into the holder, we head for the exit.

I twist and untwist the hem of my shirt in my hands. How do I bring up my past? With Lessa and Lena, the topic flows more naturally. Because they knew everything about me already. We're a family. And I've never given much thought to talking with someone else about it.

We walk through the parking lot and his hand snakes around mine. "What are you thinking right now?"

I peek up at him, working hard to school my expression, hoping it appears relaxed and casual. "I've never talked about my life with anyone except Lessa and Lena. I don't know how.

I don't want to seem like I'm putting you off or pushing you away."

"Just share what's on your mind. Tell me what you're comfortable sharing."

I stare ahead, allowing my vision to lose focus as he guides us. *Just find the words, Mags. Breathe deep and let go of your fear.* I repeat this in my head a few times, diligently working to calm my nerves. When I'm ready to speak, I pray I sound calmer than I am.

"I have a lot of sorrow in my past. Sorrow I don't make a habit of sharing with anyone. It has taken a long time for me to get to where I am today. To have some semblance of normal in my life. The way you've seen me over the last couple of days, it's not how I am on a regular day. It might seem boring to someone looking in from the outside, but I find it comforting and safe."

I watch as my words run through his mind and are processed with high precision. And I'm not sure if he's overanalyzing them or repeating them like a scratched record. So I give him time to process what I've said and leave the conversation in his court. I divulged a lot to him, more than I've given any other person. He needs time to absorb it and give me something in return. Now it's my turn to wonder what he is thinking, but I am not going to ask. Not yet.

Our silence turns soothing as we stroll through the lot. His presence is far from uncomfortable, even with the current lack of dialogue. I enjoy stillness every morning at home, but this version is different. There's a huge contrast between nature and the man beside me. And I like and fear how it all makes me feel.

"I hope, in time, you'll be at ease enough to share what has brought so much sadness into your life. I won't pry though.

The only thing I ask is, do you think you can find a place for me? In your routine, that is."

I absorb his words. I have never had to *fit* someone into my life, to create a place for them in my world.

Is that something I can do? Am I capable of that kind of change? Can I let him in? Am I willing to give up the safe-guards I've put in place?

"I don't know. I'm going to have to think about it. Can you give me time to do that?"

CHAPTER 11

GEOFFREY

Stacks of papers scatter across my desk as I turn to my laptop, my hazy eyes unable to focus on the contract or schematics in front of me. I press my palms to my eyes, mumbling to myself. "Get ahold of yourself."

It has been thirteen days since Mags and I had breakfast. Thirteen endless, treacherous days. Since that morning at Java and Teas Me, we have had three miniscule text exchanges.

GEOFFREY

Hey, how are you?

MAGDALENA

Good. You?

GEOFFREY

Good.

MAGDALENA

Sorry, I'm a little busy at work. Chat later?

GEOFFREY

Sure thing.

Each time I stare at the screen, it baffles me to see the exact same exchange all three times. It has me questioning whether or not we shared the same opinions of our last conversation.

I replay her last words to me. *Can you give me time to do that?* My response was a resounding yes. But maybe I should have asked for clarification.

I want to give her space to figure out how we can move forward. But I cannot help behaving like a needy teenager, checking my phone often for a missed call or message from her.

Something. Anything.

Yes, I could step it up a notch. Check-in with her while she is not at work. Follow up on her offer to chat later. And I want to. *So, what is holding me back?* That is a good question. And one I would love to have the answer for.

Sleeping is a joke. Every night, I lay on my bed exhausted, my eyes plastered to the ceiling, praying to get at least one solid hour of sleep. But it never comes. Restless, I watch the moonlight cast shadows along the ceiling, wishing for some form of distraction. Anything. I dream up all the possible reasons why she has not reached out.

And then my mind drifts to Charlotte. To the years we had together. How we had our whole lives mapped out. And how it was all taken away from us in the blink of an eye.

Losing her... it is the exact reason why I have steered clear of relationships. Why sex has been the only intimacy I have wanted over the last decade. Why I need to be in control. Because with Charlotte, I had zero control in the end.

Too many times, I have picked up my phone and composed

a message to Mags, only to delete it in the end. Am I a coward? I keep telling myself that I am giving her the space she wanted, the space she requested so she can figure out how all of this can work.

But why is it taking so long? Has she just tossed me to the side? Am I trash? I want to talk to her. Ask her if she has made a decision. Ask her if she wants to give what's happening between us a shot. Does it really take this long to determine if you have time for someone in your life?

God, how I want her in my life.

I will be the bigger person and give her a few more days. A few more days of sleepless nights. A few more days to sort things out on her end. A few more days...

"Dude, you look like shit."

I lift my gaze from the mountain of paperwork strewn across my desk, not even sure which client's files I have jumbled in the mess, to see Logan standing in the doorway. "Fuck off. I haven't slept much."

He inches backward, his hands coming up in surrender. "What the hell, man? Just pointing out the obvious. Take some time off. We don't have another project starting for a few weeks."

"I'd love nothing more than to take a vacation, but I need the distraction of being here. If I'm at home, it gives me too much time to think about shit that I need to be distracted from right now."

Logan sits in one of the chairs on the opposite side of my desk and drills a hole into my head with his gaze. "What's up with you? You haven't been yourself for days. Owen and I have passed it off, hoping whatever it is would end. But it hasn't."

He's put the ball in my court. I hadn't talked with either of them about Mags. What would I say? *I met this woman. She's gorgeous and generous and kind. We hooked up, sort of. I haven't heard much from her since the morning after.* In most circumstances, this would be great. But I am a fucking lost cause. I did not want or need pity from anyone.

Pressing my elbows on the desk, I lay my head in my hands. He will hold this over my head forever, teasing me for being such a girl about things, but I really do not give a shit anymore. "I met someone."

"You *met* someone?" His question hangs in the air, waiting for more input from me.

I glance up from my hands and catch his gaze, full of wonder. Not wonder as to how it happened. No, more like wondering why I look like I am at death's door if I met someone. His head tilts as he studies me, awaiting my answer.

"Yes. We had amazing chemistry." Our chemistry is beyond amazing, to be honest. I have never felt so connected to another person. Ever. Which adds another layer of undesirable emotions—guilt. Because what does that mean regarding Charlotte?

"Had? As in past tense?" His questions are laced with confusion.

"We went out for dinner, spent the night together, and then the next morning... curbside." More like in a trench, with no way to get out.

"Obviously you want more than a one-night stand with this woman. How long since you've talked?"

I am really beginning to hate this conversation. I hate that I feel lost over someone I barely know. I hate that I sound like a whiny toddler being denied the toy on the store shelf. *How did I get here? And why do I need to keep talking to Logan about it?*

"Almost two weeks. We've exchanged a few generic texts,

but nothing more. I'll message her tonight. I'd already planned on it."

He nods, deep in thought. What the hell is he thinking about? I am already tired of this conversation and want to be left alone.

"Look, man, I know I'm no expert in the relationship department, but you know Owen and I are here if you need to get anything off your chest. Or if you just want to hang. Right?" His expression is not one of pity, more like he wants to be a good friend when I am anything but.

"I know. It's just crazy. I don't know what the fuck to do. Should I have called her already? Should I just leave her alone? I've never been so indecisive in my life. I've never felt so... not myself."

I want answers. And at this point, I do not care who gives them to me. As long as I get them.

Why has she waited so long? Is she blowing me off and I can't take the hint? Or is she still interested and doesn't know how to tell me?

The vicious cycle of unanswered questions needs to end. My head is on the verge of blowing up from all the thoughts roaming within it.

"Geoff. You know you're like a brother to me. You know I'd do anything for or with you." He looks down at his lap and brushes his hands across one leg as if something is there. "I'll give you whatever advice I can. But I don't know the perfect resolution. That's only something you and her will find together."

Hanging my head in defeat, I inhale deep. Although Logan did not have all the answers, at least he listened. "Thanks for trying, man. I'll talk to her later and get everything figured out. Tomorrow will be better, I'm sure."

Logan pushes his chair back before he stands, the chair's legs scuffing along the floor. My head still drooped toward my desk, he reaches over and pats my back. It's his version of providing comfort, as he is not much of a touchy-feely type. I'm thankful for my friends, but right now... I experience no comfort.

It will get better, at least I hope it will. I am not sure if I even believe the words as they tumble out of my mouth.

Tomorrow will be better. It has to be.

CHAPTER 12

MAGDALENA

Statice seems to be overflowing. In the last week alone, we have had three new kids join the program. The word busy does not remotely cover the workweek. I love the volunteer work I do, and I wouldn't change it for anything, but this is one of those times when I wish we had more people at the center to help. I want to make sure I can devote the right amount of time to each one, but this week has brought about my biggest challenge in all the years I have been here.

"Hey, sweetheart. How ya doing?" Beatrice asks, her shoulder leaning against my office doorframe.

A half-smile lifts the corner of my lips. "I'm alright. Just reviewing the new kids' files."

She gestures to the chairs across from me, asking permission to sit. I nod, coming around to sit beside her.

When we're both seated, her hand rests over mine on my knee. "Sweetheart, I don't want you getting too overwhelmed here. If you need someone else to work with one of the kids, just say the word. It doesn't make you weak to ask for help."

I stare at our connected hands and nod. Funny how her thoughts mirror mine, and yet I can't outright agree with them. Lines sit more prominently on Beatrice's skin now versus when I met her almost nine years ago. But her touch was just as comforting then as it is now. Although she could never replace my mom, Beatrice's gentle nature often reminds me of her.

"If I need help, I promise to say something," I share. "I'm just finding my groove."

Although I had only been working at Statice for close to two months now, it felt much longer. The first year after my mom's death, I walked these halls enough to do it with my eyes shut. I resisted the program at first, in denial about what happened to my mom. But over time, Beatrice helped guide me in a better direction.

Now when I gaze at the walls and people in Statice... it's family. And Beatrice is the matriarch.

"Good, but don't you go forgetting that we're a family and we help each other," she scolds, a hint of teasing in her tone.

I press my hand over my heart. "Scout's honor, I won't forget."

She smiles her big, toothy smile and my chest warms. I lean forward and hug her. We break apart, her fingers tucking a few strands behind my ear. "There's another reason I came to see you. The paper—" She stalls a moment. "Have you thought any about the interview they want to do?"

I slump against the back of the chair. "Uh, yeah. Initially, I was going to decline. But after taking a few days to think it over, I've decided I should."

Beatrice squeezes both my hands in hers, a little too hard. "Great! They'd like to hear about Statice and the program," she hesitates but continues, "and what it's like from someone with first-hand experience."

I swallow hard. "Yeah, the journalist explained that a little. That's kind of why I asked to think about it." Inhaling deep, I continue, "But I'm working on putting myself out there more. Maybe sharing my story will help. Me or another child."

Beatrice wraps her arms around me again. "This will be good for you, sweetheart. I know some of this stuff still weighs you down."

"It does," I confirm. "But I'm trying to not let it."

"When will they do the interview?"

"After I confirmed, the journalist emailed me a list of questions. He's coming by tomorrow to take a photo."

"So, you're telling me I should wear my Saturday best tomorrow," she jokes. She gives me one last squeeze before releasing me and standing. As she walks to the door, she peers over her shoulder at me. "It's five o'clock. No more working tonight. All that paperwork will be there when you come back." And before I can answer, she walks out the door.

I gather my belongings and check my watch. If I make it home in the next fifteen minutes, I can soak in the tub a little before meeting Lessa and Lena for dinner.

Twenty minutes later, the smell of lavender wafts through the air. A cloud of bubbles grows tall in my bathtub. Turning the handles, the foam layer a couple inches below the faucet, I ease into the glorious hot water and relax as my muscles loosen.

I love giving back to those kids, supporting them in every possible way, but I need time to decompress from it all. Many of the days were an emotional overload. Hearing their stories, understanding what they are dealing with now, hearing their heartache... I couldn't help but dredge up all the memories of my parents and how my life changed so radically with their deaths. It is especially difficult when someone else's circumstances are similar to my own.

I lay my head back and close my eyes and shut out everything. No work. No center. No walks down memory lane. I need this, a little bit of time to reset myself before meeting up with Lessa and Lena for dinner. I am in dire need of girl's night tonight. The weight of so many others sat on my shoulders, a burden only my best friends could help alleviate.

The chime from my phone jolts me as I begin drifting off to sleep. Falling asleep in the tub isn't an abnormal occurrence for me, the long days at Statice wiping out every ounce of my energy. I'm both thankful and unhappy someone brought me back to the present.

Grabbing my phone from the counter, I assume Lessa is messaging me, like she did every Friday, double-checking to see I am meeting them. It isn't Lessa. It isn't Lena, either. It's Geoff.

Guilt washes over me, and it is huge. When we left the coffee shop a couple weeks ago, I took the possibility of us having more into my hands. I told him I needed time to figure it all out. How to fit him into my life. How to fit him into my routine. I was responsible for the next step that we took.

And I failed. Big time.

I have been so wrapped up in everything and anything at the center that I hadn't thought about him, or us, once. For that, I am a horrible human. Somehow, some way, I had to make this up to him. And to apologize to him for not reaching out to him sooner.

GEOFFREY

Just wanted to say hi and see how you were.

MAGDALENA

Hey Geoff I feel like a total jerk right now. I've been so busy at Statice. Sorry I didn't message sooner.

My eyes are glued to the screen of my phone, waiting for that little magic bubble to pop up and indicate he is responding to me. Seconds tick by with nothing happening. After a minute, or so, my unspoken wish comes true, and three dots appear.

GEOFFREY

No worries. How are you?

Confusion fills the space around me. Five simple words. Maybe it's just me, but his response seems a little lackluster considering the guy he resembled weeks ago. This response is flat. Forced. Like he doesn't know what to say to me, but wanted to say something. Small talk to keep the conversation going. Maybe he has had a lot going on too. Hopefully that is all it is.

MAGDALENA

I'm okay. Statice has been bombarded the last week. I feel like I haven't even had time to breathe.

GEOFFREY

Sorry to hear it's been so crazy. Hopefully it'll get better soon.

Okay, something is definitely off. I have been around people enough at Statice to pinpoint when someone is feeling down. The Geoff I met, the Geoff I was intimate with, didn't seem like someone who would make idle chit-chat or a conversation without purpose. And that is what this is. A conversation without meaning. *Is it because I haven't given him a response about us yet?*

> MAGDALENA
>
> How are you? I really am sorry I haven't messaged or called. Forgive me?

> GEOFFREY
>
> Forgiven. I'm alright. Work has been slow for me – not starting another project for a few weeks. Just been doing whatever.

Doing whatever? What the hell is that? Geoff doesn't come off as a person who does *whatever*. I need to see him. Talk with him, face to face. If there is one thing I really don't like about messaging, it is the fact that you can't tell the emotion of the person on the other end. How it's deciphered is entirely up to the recipient. And right now, my decoder ring is malfunctioning.

> MAGDALENA
>
> So I'm meeting up with Lessa & Lena in a little bit for dinner, but I'd love to see you later. Tonight or tomorrow? What's better for you?

My phone doesn't show him answering me for a minute or two, so I set it back down, drain the too short bath and start getting ready for dinner. Five minutes later, my phone chimes again.

> GEOFFREY
>
> Tonight. Can you come by after dinner?

If anyone could see my face right now... The length of time residing between my message and his was far too long for such an abrupt answer. I don't quite know what to think. *Did he not want to see me?* Pushing that thought out of my head, I respond.

MAGDALENA

Yes. Send me your address & I'll message you when I'm headed your way.

A moment later, his address flashes onto my screen, and I can't help the flurry of anxiety I feel. What will I say to him? I left him hanging for weeks and, most of that time, I didn't even figure out how to make a relationship with him work. Time to cram an all-night study session into the next couple of hours.

Here's to hoping I figure it all out.

CHAPTER 13

GEOFFREY

I am breathless after spending the last hour and a half power cleaning my house. The moment Mags offered to come over, I rushed to clean my slovenly bachelor pad.

There is a light knock at my door. I inhale several deep breaths and walk to the foyer. I gaze over at the mirror in the entryway and check over my appearance before opening the door.

I turn the handle and air fills my lungs for the first time in days. The sight of her lights a fire in my chest. *God, she is beautiful.* More so now than before. For a moment, I allow myself to be lured in by her steely eyes and simmer in the connection we share.

She also seems a little mesmerized, the notion dousing the fire in my chest with gasoline. As much as I blaze for her, I am also at ease with her. *How can an inferno soothe someone?*

"Hey…" Her soft voice carries across my skin and sinks deep inside.

I open the door a little further and step aside. "Hi. How

"It was good. It's always good. That place consistently amazes me."

Cheryl told me Mags was in the restaurant every Friday, but Mags doesn't know I am privy to such information. And I want it to remain that way. "Where? Black Silk?"

"Yeah, we go there every week and catch up."

"That's cool. I don't really hang with Logan and Owen much. Our work schedule kind of makes it difficult." Between the three of us, one of us is always bogged down with a project. It was seldom when we were all at a point where we felt comfortable doing anything outside of those four walls.

"That sucks. I don't know what I'd do if I didn't have Lessa and Lena and our time together. It's like therapy for me."

She stands less than two feet away, a little fidgety and eyes darting around the room. It is in this moment I realize we had not moved out of the foyer. The fact that she is in front of me again thoroughly sidetracks me and I am an idiot for leaving us both standing here.

"I'm sorry, come in. I didn't intend for us to stand by the door the whole time."

With a light laugh, she follows me to the living room. I sit on the couch and give her a choice to sit by me or in one of the chairs. Relief fills my chest when she opts to sit next to me. It is incomprehensible the way this woman makes my heart race. And I am not going to lie, it is also a bit disarming.

"Did you want a drink? Water?"

"No, I'm okay. Thanks, though."

I nod and fall silent. I want her to initiate the conversation. After all, she is the one who wanted time to think over things. The one who needed to sort out how we could fit into her world.

A few minutes of quiet stretch between us and I wonder if

she is going to say anything at all. I take a deep breath and prepare to speak, to say anything, and get what I want to hear out in the air.

And then her voice floats in the air between us.

"Geoff, I really am sorry I didn't talk to you sooner. I was so busy at the center, especially in the last week. I didn't even have time for myself. It was pretty much a crazy cycle of no downtime. It wasn't my intention to leave you hanging for so long."

This is good news, right? She wanted to talk to me sooner but was too distracted by work and too tired to do anything. This brings me one step closer to happy.

"I get it. Sometimes work is like that for me, too. I get so wrapped up in a project, I forget what day of the week it is. I can't tell you how many times I've gone all day without eating."

Hopefully, I relieve some of the tension between us by letting her know I understand. But at the same time, no joke, I missed her on an unhealthy level. I mean, I barely know her.

And yet, she is the antidote to everything that ails me.

"Thanks for understanding. Although, I feel like I need to apologize a million more times."

"Please don't. Really, I get it."

I want us past the apologies. I want us to start talking about how she could work us into her life, but another pause hits us like a wall of humidity.

We sit there, both apparently unknowing of what to do or say. So I excuse myself for a minute and go to the kitchen to grab some water. As I fill the glass, I swear to myself that I will provoke the words I need to hear, if she doesn't volunteer them. One of us needs to get this off and running. If she isn't going to, I would.

All I need is to know where her head is at. Does she want more?

When I make my way back into the room, I spare a moment to take all of her in. Her hands rest in her lap, fingers continually moving, fiddling with everything and nothing, her eyes trailing her own movements. She's nervous. And she isn't aware I have walked back into the room.

"What's weighing so heavy on your mind?"

Her eyes pop up, the corner of her lip drawn in by her teeth. "I was just thinking about how much I like you. That I'd like to figure out a way that we can spend time together. Without disrupting our lives."

I walk back to the couch and resume my place beside her. "I really like you, too. I'd love nothing more than to spend more time together."

Her smile brightens her features and awakens something deep in my core, penetrating the depths of my soul. Without a doubt in my mind, or my heart, I would do anything for this woman.

"The first thing I want to say is how much I want this to work between us. There's not a time I remember wanting something so much." Her hazel eyes rimmed with evergreen study me, her voice soft.

I make every effort to not come across as a jerk or an idiot. "Okay. What exactly does that mean?"

She needs to spell it out for me. I don't want to assume anything. She should be the one to set up the parameters so she is comfortable with us. Because that is all that matters. Us.

"I guess it means I want to find a way for us to be more, without compromising everything else. For you or me. I wasn't kidding when I said I do the same thing every day, with a couple exceptions. And although I've stepped out of my comfort zone a little recently, I've structured my life so I have a solid foundation. A fortress. Something that was taken away from me at one time."

I am dying to ask her what she means, but I won't. She needs more time to get to know me better. To trust me. Then she will tell me why her life is so set in stone. So restricted.

"It's not my intention to change anything about you. You tell me how we move forward. However you need to do this is how we will. You lead, and I will follow. All I want is you. As long as I have that, I will do this, you and me," I gesture between us, "whichever way you need me to."

With that, her face softens and displays a hint of sympathy. It should be obvious I am willing to bend and flex to her needs, if that is what it takes to be in a relationship with her.

"Give me a minute."

She sits unmoving, gazing into my eyes and seeing something much deeper. Processing everything we both said. I can practically see the cogs turning in her head. She is trying to figure out the how and the when and the where. I grant her request and don't interrupt.

She reaches for my hand, gripping it light in her own. Both of us bow our heads toward the gentle gesture, then come back to each other. My chest clenches, a sudden tightness tugging from every direction. Fuck, I want this. A relationship with her. I want it more than food or water or oxygen. She's a part of me, a part I never knew existed or was missing.

"We need to start kind of slow. See each other for two or three weeks before we take things to the next level. And I know that's somewhat of a contradiction, considering we've already been intimate, but I need us to ease into our relationship before sex reenters the equation. I need you to understand things will probably be different for us than anyone else's relationship, until I know I'm okay. Can you be patient with me?"

If patience is what she requires, then I will be more than happy to grant her wish. "Yes, I can. You may need to guide me, Mags."

"I want to see you, but maybe we'll do a few nights a week for a little bit. Okay? Till we get into the groove of us," she voices. I doubt she has as many questions as me.

Some might say we were setting up some sort of contractual relationship. Setting specifics in writing, so to speak. But I don't care. I had not seen her in weeks, and she is gifting me with multiple days a week. I stow my excitement, answering her as calm as I can muster. "I'm good with that. Did you have certain days in mind?"

"Fridays I always go out with Lessa and Lena. Maybe we can do Monday, Wednesday, and Saturday. Spread it out during the week." Her eyes question the days more than her words, her teeth troubling her lip once more.

I don't want to sound over-eager to answer her, but I am. Elated at the fact this is happening. That this moment is real. I want to stick to her pace, but announce to the world my excitement. Dating had never been my thing, but I couldn't wait to hear all of Mags' stories. As calm as possible, I answer. "Sounds perfect. We can have dinner on the weeknights if that's okay with you. On Saturdays, though, I'd like to do something more. Like a movie or bowling, anything, plus dinner."

Her face lights up, and I mirror the expression. "I love it! I actually haven't done too much, so everything will be like a new experience."

Exultation courses through my veins. Although our relationship is starting out quite untraditionally, I don't care. If Mags is in my world, that is the only thing that matters.

"I'm glad I will be the one to experience them with you."

We sit comfortably, content, our fingers entwined, eyes locked, a pleasant stillness surrounding us.

Before long, she breaks the serenity encasing us. "I think I should go."

Why? I stop myself from asking. I don't want her to leave. Not yet. She's only been here for a fraction of time. Even if we just stay together on the couch—saying nothing, doing nothing—I crave her presence. But alas, I know I should cede to her wishes. After all, she has rewarded me with the most wonderful of gifts tonight. Her.

Reluctantly, I rise to my feet, her hand still wrapped in mine, standing her up beside me. "Let me walk you out."

On our way to her car, not a word is spoken, the two of us walking hand-in-hand. She pauses at her car door, pressing the fob button to unlock it. She seems caught up in her own thoughts, her eyes staring through the glass of her driver's side door. Opting to break her reverie, I reach in front of her, yanking the handle and opening her door.

Her gaze switches from the car to me, her eyes studying mine. Her face is scattered with indecision, about what I'm unsure, and panic creeps into my chest. Is she having doubts already? I don't think I can handle another fall. Not so soon.

Stuck in my own cloud of worry, I don't feel the shift in mood until her lips are on mine. Lavishing me. Consuming me. Her desire spilling over and flooding me.

I could kiss her forever.

CHAPTER 14

MAGDALENA

Steam wafts from the mug resting between my palms, the perfume from the jasmine-green tea has my mouth watering. I bring the cup to my lips, the scalding liquid searing my tongue. I set the mug on the side table and decide to let it cool for a bit.

My eyes drift beyond my yard, the tree line fading to a fuzzy, green blob of foliage as my mind wanders to the night before. So much of last night feels like a dream. After I left the restaurant, my brain was a scrambled mess. I had no idea what to say to Geoff. But the moment he opened the door... None of it mattered.

We stood at the entrance of his home, eyes locked, and I fumbled over how to commit to a romantic relationship. It wasn't as if I didn't want to be with him. More like I didn't know if I could actually take the leap. Dating wasn't an anomaly; it just hadn't worked in my favor for years. But I shocked myself, and him, when I professed my feelings. Honestly, he probably expected me to shut down the idea. Especially after

"I have a boyfriend," I mutter.

Times like this, I miss Mom. I may be in my mid-twenties, but I never had her long enough to discuss relationships and heartbreak. Mom was alive when I dated my first boyfriend, but we didn't get to have the long talks I would've liked. I guess I thought she'd always be around. That I could wait to ask her all my questions and share my feelings. But I was wrong.

Sure, I had Beatrice. And we shared some of these moments. But it wasn't the same. And as much as I try not to live or dwell in the past, moments like this make it a little tough.

Before Dad had his stroke, I dated a few guys. One guy stuck around for a month—things were good until he made an adverse comment about my 'skills' in the bedroom. As for the other two, they didn't pan out past the first or second date. Since Dad's stroke and eventual passing, dating was the lowest priority.

It's sad, but the last time I remember having an actual relationship is high school. Can I even call it a relationship, since I was fifteen?

My high school boyfriend broke up with me after only a month and a half of dating. We had slept together a couple times, but he wanted a girl who would give it up all the time. Sadly, this was the longest relationship I'd ever had. That fact bothered me and didn't at the same time.

At the time of our breakup, I was so upset. *Why did the boys only want girls who put out? Was that the only thing they wanted in life? Sex?*

After we broke up, I kept to myself at school. I didn't feel any desire to be social with anyone. I didn't have it in me to fake some form of happiness. Outside of school, I spent time with my parents and my girlfriends. Family was always the best remedy, and I was fortunate to have the most amazing people in my inner circle.

Three weeks passed by and it finally felt as if I was getting back to a better place. Back to the old me. My parents had been giving me more time than most teenagers enjoyed. But I was not like most teenage girls, and I absorbed every hug, laugh, and joke. Little did I know, those precious moments with my parents would soon come to a dead end.

It was less than two weeks before Christmas. Dad and I had been home, waiting for Mom to walk through the front door from work. But she was late. Much later than usual. Dad and I were getting everything ready for dinner when the call came in.

Mom had been in a head-on collision with a drunk driver and died at the scene of the accident.

That day shifted our world. After that moment, the only guy I cared about was my dad. Everything and anything to do with boyfriends vanished. Dad and I became practically inseparable, except for work and school.

Dad was such a stronghold for me. He had so much to deal with—not just emotionally, but mentally, physically, and financially, as well. I couldn't even imagine what it had been like for him to lose his wife. He had known her much longer than I had and they'd had a bond that even I couldn't comprehend.

Losing Mom changed us both. We did everything for each other, without question, knowing that life was precious. I loved my dad with every fiber of my being.

Then, fate dug her nails in me again.

The second semester of my sophomore year, college was in full swing. As was winter, the snow setting records one day to the next. I still lived at home rather than the dorms. Thankfully, most of my drive home was on the highway and the snow wasn't a bother.

After finishing a study session, I messaged Dad to let him know I was headed home. He messaged back to let me know he needed to stop at the grocery store after work, but wouldn't be long.

On his short drive home, he had a stroke.

His car smashed into a tree, and he was rushed to the emergency room after the paramedics arrived. When I spoke with the doctor tending to his care, he said my dad had a fifty-fifty chance of survival and we would have to wait and see how his body responded to care.

After countless hours of monitoring, Dad was released from the hospital. But home was never the same. For the first few months, nurses came by and tended to him. They guided me as to the care he needed, and eventually I assumed the role of nurse. Actual nurses still checked in, but they were far and few between.

My world stopped spinning that day. I attended college online. And I only left the house when someone came by to monitor him. Although I earned my degree, I never walked across the stage or shook hands with the dean. Being on that stage just wasn't important.

I shake my head, trying to dissolve the sad memories seeping their way so into the present. The evergreens and oaks in my back yard come back into focus, the sun's brilliant beams highlighting every branch, leaf, and needle. Sitting on my lounger is therapy. It's the perfect place to lose and find myself. And I'm safe here.

Sometimes guilt lingers when I suppress the memories of

my parents, but I don't want to dishonor them. Their memory shouldn't consist of how they died, but of how they lived. I cherish the happy memories. The scent of Mom's perfume. How she could light up a room shrouded in darkness. How she was my best friend. My dad's smile, primarily when my mom was nearby. The way he could turn a fridge full of nothing into the best meal you'd ever eaten. And his hugs. God, he gave the best hugs. They were a mix of a warm blanket and musky pine and love.

Those little tidbits. Those fragile snippets. That is what I ache to hold onto for dear life.

My parents would have been proud of what I've done, giving part of myself to others who need it most. But I think they would also be sad knowing I have shut part of myself away. That I have suppressed the best parts of myself.

For them, and for myself, I'm broadening my horizons. I'm stepping out into the world. Doing normal things with my friends and my *boyfriend*. Experiencing all life has to offer. And experiencing life with someone at my side. Being in a relationship is surreal. I know things will be different, but I have to start somewhere, and I am tired of living like a robot.

I bring my mug back to my lips, the tea no longer blistering hot. As ruled by routine as my life has been, it is time I break the mold. The past will always be a part of who I am, none of which can be changed. But the future... So much potential lingers before me. Potential I am robbing myself of.

Kicking my legs off the lounger, I walk inside and stare around the room. The furniture and décor haven't changed since I was a child. If I want to stop living in the past, it is time to make some changes.

The first change... discovering the new me.

After spending several hours wandering around Olympia, I picked out some new things for my bedroom, the living room, and the guest room. Nothing over the top—bedding, new throw pillows and blankets, artwork.

I stripped the beds and donned the new bedding. Gone were the outdated floral quilts. Now, fluffy heather gray comforters reside, a pinch pleat adding texture. Next, I swapped out the framed art on the walls, replacing flowers with colorful images of Buddha and pagodas.

The only art I didn't remove was a set of three canvases in the living room. Oil paintings of ballerinas—one monochrome, one sepia, and the last brilliant in color. They remind me of Mom and our shared love for ballet.

As I shuffle around the living room, adding the final touches, realization hits. Today is Saturday. Last night, I told Geoff we would see each other on Saturdays.

Should I call or message him? Has he thought about us going out tonight?

The momentum I've had for the last five hours takes a nosedive. Will going on dates always be this nerve-wracking? God, I hope not. Maybe my nervousness stems from my limited experience. Plus, our first date was quite intense. Will they all be like that?

Maybe we can do something more normal, like dinner and a movie. I haven't been in a movie theater in who knows how long. And I haven't the slightest idea what's playing. But miscellaneous boxed candies, greasy popcorn, and us—it sounds like the perfect combination.

For a second date, one that will resemble more of a first,

this sounds like a perfect plan. No longer able to keep the plans to myself, I pick up my phone and type out a message to Geoff.

MAGDALENA

Hey So I was thinking maybe we could do dinner & a movie tonight. Thoughts?

GEOFFREY

Sounds great. Anything striking your mood for either?

MAGDALENA

Oooh! How about sushi? I have no idea what movies are out. You pick.

GEOFFREY

Any type of movies you don't like?

I ponder this a moment. I'll watch just about anything. But what do you watch on your second date with someone?

MAGDALENA

Nothing too gory or too sappy. Everything else is fair game.

GEOFFREY

Got it. How about if I pick you up around 4:30?

MAGDALENA

Sounds like a plan

Thrill courses through my veins and energizes me anew. *Holy shit.* Date night. With my boyfriend.

A light sheen pierces my skin, my palms shaking slightly. *Take a deep breath, Mags. You can do this. Just be yourself.*

What the hell do I do now? Clothes. I need to figure out what to wear. Are movie theaters still cold? I walk over to my closet, the clothing-covered hangers taunting me.

I check my watch—it's already two o'clock. I have less than three hours to get myself put together and become a bit saner. *Deep breaths, Mags. This is normal. Dates with people you like are a good thing.*

CHAPTER 15

GEOFFREY

My fingers tighten around the leather-encased steering wheel, my eyes landing on Mags' Audi parked in the driveway in front of me.

The clock on the dash reads four-twenty-eight. I have been sitting here for the last five minutes, swimming in her words from last night, remembering every nervous twitch she made. She was so worried. But so was I. I still am. How can I not be? It's obvious I'm getting ahead of myself, but I can't help it.

I step out, heading up the path to her doorway, the small lights on either side lit up. There is still a bit of time between now and sunset, but the lights must be on a sensor, the front of her house shaded by a mass of trees on the sloping mountainside behind her house. Reaching the door, my hand hovers a few seconds before landing a soft knock on the wood.

When the door opens, I am greeted by the sight of pure beauty. No matter how many times I have laid eyes on her, she consistently steals my breath each and every time. Mags has this way about her, one that makes casual look classy. It isn't a look many women can pull off, especially younger women. She mesmerizes me at every turn.

"Hey there, beautiful. You ready to go?"

"Yeah. Let me just grab my jacket. It's been a while since I've been in a theater, but I'm sure they're still chilly."

Gravel crunches under our feet as we walk to my car. Following her to the passenger side, I open the door, gesturing her to get in.

"Thank you."

Attempting to keep my grin somewhat contained, I return the sentiment. "You're most welcome." With her, I can't help myself.

Mags makes me want to be more than just a guy going out with a girl. She makes me want to be a better person. To be kinder. To open up. To be vulnerable. Maybe it's her selfless nature and desire to help others. Or oddly enough, maybe Mags reminds me of Charlotte. Not in appearance, but her demeanor. Both of them reserved in some ways, yet gregarious in others—dependent on their surroundings. Both of them open and honest and not afraid to speak what's on their mind. It's a refreshing quality. But one difference between Charlotte and Mags—their drive.

Charlotte had drive, but it was only for herself and the goals she wanted to accomplish. Mags, though... her drive revolves around others. Her selfless nature is her most attractive quality. Not that Charlotte was never selfless—it just wasn't first nature for her. She was her number one priority. Whereas with Mags, everyone else comes before her.

Mags is the first woman since Charlotte, who gives me hope. Hope for a future where I won't be sitting in an empty house all alone, but traveling with someone by my side. Hope for the life and family I dreamt of years ago. The pitter-patter of little feet running through the house. The opportunity to grow old with someone who means the world to me.

I may have been a manwhore the last several years—bedding countless women to forget what I lost with Charlotte. I assumed that would be the extent of my life in the "relationship" department. But from the moment I laid eyes on Mags, I knew she was different. The fissures in my heart slowly stitching together.

There's no simple way to pinpoint the main source of what makes Mags different from all the other women I've been with. Maybe it's just an energy I sense when she's nearby. Or perhaps it's the universe's way of giving me a second chance at love. Repayment for the loss and suffering I endured in the past.

It will be a long time before my heart is whole again. But every moment I spend with Mags heals wounds I never thought would close.

I slide into the driver's seat and start up the car. Before arriving at Mags' house, I'd memorized the route from her home to the sushi restaurant. I could have easily used the map on my phone for navigation, but the last thing I wanted was the robot directions interrupting any conversation we may have.

A moment later, we're headed in the direction of J's Sushi Bar & Restaurant. It is, by far, the best casual sushi and Japanese restaurant in the area. I am not sure if she has been there before, but I'm excited to share one of my favorite places with her.

"So where have you gotten sushi at before?"

Her eyes shift from the row of houses outside her window to mine, amused by my inquiry. "So here comes my inner sheltered self. I've really only had sushi from that little spot in the grocery store. I know, I'm adventurous." She lifts her hands to either side of her face, palms out and making some sort of dazzling gesture.

Laughter erupts from her, the sound light and musical. I can't help but join in. Listening to her laugh did strange things to me, and I make a mental note to lock the light-hearted sound away in my memory bank. That singular sound, I want it to reverberate from her lips often, and I want to be the reason it does.

"At least it's a start. Although, I should warn you. After you eat tonight's sushi, the grocery store stuff will never be the same."

"Setting the bar for me, huh?" Her left brow cocks up.

"It's not really me setting the bar, but I'll take some credit."

"So where are we going?"

In some ways, I love that she hasn't experienced too much of the town. It makes every place new and exciting again. "It's a surprise."

Sharing J's with Mags has been better than I could have imagined. Great conversation. Lots of laughter. And eating until we could eat no more. Fantastic.

We didn't just share great food and conversation. But also small parts of ourselves.

When Mags said, "Take something I love, dip it in batter and throw it in a fryer. That's the way to my heart," I about lost it. Several patrons burned me with their judgmental eyes as I laughed too loud, but I ignored them. I had never known a woman who openly admitted their love of fried foods.

Her honesty is a refreshing change.

And when a piece of sushi slipped from my chopsticks and made soy sauce art on my shirt, I shrugged it off while she muffled her laughter. Little did she know, I planned to keep the stained shirt as is.

We talked about work. About friends. About music. She gave me so much of herself tonight, and I am so grateful. From the few times we've been together, I observed a difference in her tonight. It isn't dramatic, but it is there. And I like it.

We grab our leftover packages and head for the exit, thanking the sushi chef on our way out. A tradition I picked up on when I watched others leaving and doing the same. The sushi chef waves goodbye to us, and thanks me by name. *Yeah, I am here a lot.*

We approach the car and I open the door for Mags. She gives me her brilliant smile and slips into the passenger seat. Her smile incomparable. Every time I make her lips curve upward, I capture the moment in my mind and stow it away for safekeeping.

A short drive down the road, I park the car a block from the theater. Mags looks at me confused. "We still have another thirty minutes before the movie starts," I tell her.

When we meet at the front of the car, I snake my fingers in hers and lead her through the small park in front of us. We stroll along a wide path, gravel crunching under our feet. After a couple minutes, we step under a gazebo and sit under twinkling lights.

"I've had a really great time so far," I state.

She shifts her eyes from our locked hands and hones in on mine. "Me too," she whispers, as if she is scared to say it too loud.

"Everything okay?" *I didn't do anything wrong, did I?*

She opens her mouth, then shuts it. I don't rush her, but

notice when she puts her free hand on my knee. My knee which started bouncing sometime in the last minute.

"I'm fine. Everything is fine," she says. And instantly, I don't like the word *fine*. It is something said when a person isn't able to define how they feel—good or bad. "I guess I'm still nervous, is all."

Nervous is something I can handle. I brush my thumb over her cheek. "As long as you're okay."

She nods.

Thankfully, the mood turns less solemn and we sit under the twinkling lights of the gazebo, chatting for the next fifteen minutes. The entire time, her hand remains on my knee. It may be a simple gesture, but it means so much to me.

We leave the park hand-in-hand and amble past storefronts, the town not overly crowded for a Saturday evening. Couples and families meander. Friends share jokes and laughter. And seeing so many beaming smiles has me remembering how much I really love it here.

"So what movie are we seeing?" Mags asks.

I smirk. "You feeling like some action?"

CHAPTER 16

MAGDALENA

Initially, I told Geoff no romance or gruesome movies. I said no gore because I didn't want to be freaked out, basically jumping in his lap to be rescued. I said no romance for two reasons. One—romance is not always on a guy's top favorites list. Two—too much sappiness too soon could have one, or both, of us in some awkward state of how to proceed after the movie ends. So, we saw an action/suspense movie.

The better choice, right?

Wrong.

Don't get me wrong, the movie itself is good. I would watch it again. But some of the suspense plots had me so on edge. My heart pounding, knuckles white, my eyes glued to the screen. I wouldn't be surprised if, at some point, I'd cut the circulation off in Geoff's hand… more than once.

No matter how hard I'd tried, I couldn't keep my composure. Just as the movie seemed to settle down, a new twist was thrown into the mix. By the end of the film, I'm sure he was relieved to no longer feel my sweaty palms on his own and overjoyed to have blood flowing into all of his fingers.

The credits scroll up the screen as we head for the theater exit, and I stuff my ticket stub inside my purse. Something to remember our date with.

Passing through the oversized doors, he reaches for my hand. Without hesitation, I reciprocate. We still have a lot to learn about one another, one of those things being the forms of intimacy we find comfortable. Although we'd shared one of the most intimate nights I've ever experienced, we still didn't know that side of each other well.

"So, what'd you think about the movie?"

"It was great. I don't think I've watched something that's made my palms sweat like that in a really long time. It was a definite rush," I relay.

"I'm glad you enjoyed it. I was somewhat worried whether or not you'd like it."

"You chose well. I'm sorry about your hand. I hope I didn't break anything," I say, a grimace morphing my face into some strange combination of *eek* and *oops*.

"You can stop with the face, although it's kind of cute. As soon as I could feel my hand again, I discovered all is fine."

Our fingers still laced together, I give a little squeeze to do my own check, seeing if everything is in place. Five fingers, their shape, and size all the way they should be. Perfect and warm.

"I didn't think I'd be so freaked out in that kind of movie. That's why I said nothing gory or sappy."

"I guess you never know how it'll go. It all depends on the movie and who wrote it, that's what I say anyway."

"I suppose you're right. If we all knew what was going to happen, we wouldn't pay to go see it."

"Exactly."

We pull into my driveway, the car silent in the background, neither of us speaking a word. I have no clue what he's thinking. The not-knowing making me crazy. I want to ask him. Blurt out the question. And have him tell me all the ways he cares about me.

This feels like high school all over again. Being brought home by the boy I like and wondering what's going to happen next. *Will he kiss me? Will he want to come inside? Does he like me like I like him?*

So many questions rattle around in my brain, and I'm pretty sure the exact same thing is happening to him. I'd give him time. Time to think. Granting myself the exact same thing in return.

Do I want to kiss him? Without question, yes. I can't imagine not kissing him again. And often.

Do I want him to come inside? I do, but at the same time, I don't. After our first date, I'm still surprised at myself for letting things progress at such a rapid pace.

There's no denying how unforgettable that night had been. It was amazing on so many levels. And it superseded every other intimate experience I've had. I look forward to future repeats. But I don't want one of those days to be today. Or even the next date we go on. I need things to slow down. To be *traditional*, whatever that means. Maybe a couple more times. Gauge how we really feel before we consider that magnitude of intimacy again.

The silence of the car is broken when he opens his door. As

ever the gentleman, he walks around to my side and opens the door for me. Every gesture plucks a new heartstring and has me swooning for him further. For me, his gestures will never be undesirable.

"Thank you."

"My pleasure."

As we approach the pathway leading off the drive, his hand lands on the small of my back. For an entirely different reason this evening, adrenaline spikes my bloodstream. My skin layering in a light sheen, displaying the evidence of the rush of heat coursing through me. My lungs tight, working to draw more breath into their cavities. The pressure to alleviate the sensation has me on the verge of panting.

Please don't let me be panting.

When we reach the door, I freeze, staring at the elusive keyhole. My head and my heart waging war with one another, battling over whether or not I should ask him to come inside. I know I've already decided on this subject, but my hormones have flown off the radar and are swaying my thoughts.

I slide the key through the teeth of the lock, turning it without hurry. Silence surrounds us in a bubble once more. My eyes burning a hole through the door while staring at the knob. Geoff stands behind me, and I can feel the heat of his stare as he watches my every move.

Attempting to remain poised, I drag in a labored breath and turn to face him. When he comes into view, I lose my composure. *God, he's gorgeous.* My eyes travel up his chest, stopping when they catch sight of his Caribbean irises. My heart bangs in my chest as if I've finished the hundred-meter dash with the gold medal. I could drown in the sea of his eyes. Would I ever tire of their depth?

I wish I knew what was going on in his head. Is he struggling just the same? If he is, he masks it well. "I had a really great time tonight."

"I'm glad. I had a great time, too." His lips forming this small pucker when he says the word *too*.

If our sexual tension were a cloud, nothing would be visible for miles. I'm unsure I'll be capable of pacing our relationship. Flashes of our first night together play through my mind like a projector on a screen.

I want him again. Desperately. Now.

On the verge of sharing every ramped thought I'm having, he stops me. My breath hitches when his warm hands graze my hips. He leans into me, eyes never leaving my lips. I close my eyes, my pulse skyrocketing, my body crying out for relief. Begging as his chest brushes my breasts.

And then his lips press against mine.

Soft, warm lips graze the corner of my mouth, silently asking permission for more. I reciprocate, my wordless response granting him consent. A heartbeat later, the kiss intensifies. He pulls me closer, his arms wrapping around my waist and behind my neck. My hands clutching his biceps, needing the extra stability as my head starts to spin.

His tongue sweeps across my lips, the simple stroke has my lips parting, allowing him to deepen the kiss. I hadn't really kissed many guys in my past. Of all the kisses I'd ever experienced, none of them compare to the intensity when Geoff kisses me. The passion he exudes, that he draws out of me, reaches deep into my core, into a place I didn't realize existed, awakening parts of me I never knew were sleeping. It's raw and carnal and like nothing I have known before.

I want more. I need more.

Our tongues dance with one another, a rhythm only they know together. This moment—him, me, us—I never want it to end. I can't allow it to end. I grasp his arms tighter, pulling our bodies closer—if that's possible. The feel of him, the taste of him... complete intoxication.

As if he can hear my thoughts, his lips slow their endeavor and give way to a gentle, soft peck. Our lips meet a few more times before he slides his hands down and gives my hips a faint squeeze. The air between us cools, and I know, somehow, he manages to shift himself away from me.

Albeit quiet, I'm panting for breath, sharing the effect his lips have on me. This man knows how to make my body crave and act like no one before him. Being with him is comparable to racing in a marathon. One second, I'd been sprinting for the finish line, and the next I'd won the prize.

My eyes drift open, lock with his and become completely engulfed by his fixation. The intensity between us pivoting higher with each breath we share. The concupiscent expression on his face heightens with the change in his Caribbean blues. If I thought I could get lost in his eyes earlier, consider me now on a deserted island. Icy blue encased in a bold, navy border.

I am utterly hopeless.

"God, I really want to invite you in." The words escape my lips before I can stop them. But I'm also glad I expressed my thoughts with him.

"I know, and I understand why you aren't."

"Geoff..."

"Really. It's okay. You don't need to explain."

"We started off pretty intense. I just need us to dial it back for a little bit. I want to know you more before we dive back into the deep end."

"Charlotte, I swear, you don't need to explain yourself. When you're ready, you'll let me know. With you, I can wait. I will wait. So, please don't feel pressured to do anything you're not ready for."

I freeze, my chest constricting. And for a split-second, I want to shake my head in disbelief. *Did he just call me Charlotte?* Suddenly, I can't breathe. And it has nothing to do with the way he was kissing me seconds ago.

His eyes widen, no doubt my reaction sinking in. I watch as his eyes dart back and forth between mine, scared. He should be scared. If I were him, I would be.

I step back from him and wrap my arms around my midsection. "Who is Charlotte?"

He steps closer and I press myself flush to the door. It's odd to want him so close and nowhere near me at the same time. His head sinks and he takes a step back, stuffing his hands in his pockets. "She's no one." There is no emotion in his voice. Not despair or shame or guilt. It's just flat.

Who calls their girlfriend by the wrong name, then brushes it under the rug? He acts as if this sort of thing happens on a regular basis. As if it bears no importance. And that... it angers me.

"I think you should go," I state, opening the door behind me.

He peeks up at me. Guilt and shame, and something I can't place, tugs at his expression. "I'm sorry, Mags. It was an accident." This time the inflection is there. His worry radiating off him.

At a loss of what to say or do, I back into my foyer. "Just go home, Geoff. We will talk about this later." Because I don't have it in me to talk about it now. Not while my heart cries an endless stream of tears and my brain stomps around with clenched fists.

He winces as if I'd slapped him across the face. "Sweet dreams, Mags."

I shake my head. "Goodnight." And I shut the door just before the first tear rolls down my cheek.

CHAPTER 17

GEOFFREY

The sun wakes me the next morning, my energy drained from last night's mistake. After hours of no sleep, I resolve to fix this before the day ends. The part that surprises me the most… I hadn't said Charlotte's name aloud in almost a decade. And the time I do, I choose the worst possible time.

Sitting up in my bed, I peer out the window and catch glimpses of sunlight, watching as it plays games with the trees and scatters beams in various directions. Mags has invigorated my life. Being with her is like breathing for the first time. As if lifting a veil and exposing me to a world long forgotten. Experiencing life anew.

But last night, I screwed up. Huge.

As soon as she shut the door in my face, I wanted to explain myself. Explain who Charlotte was. Tell Mags every sorted detail of my past. Expose a piece of myself I swore would never see the light of day again.

But I left, my head and heart aching from my error.

Today, though... It is a new day. A new opportunity to make things right. A second chance to be a better person.

Snagging my phone from the charger, I type out a message to Mags.

GEOFFREY

> I'm really sorry how last night ended. If you'll give me the chance, I'd like to explain who Charlotte was.

A minute later, my phone pings. My stomach in knots before I open the message.

MAGDALENA

> This has eaten away at me all night. So, to satiate my curiosity, please share.

I inhale, my fingers hovering over the screen. How can I explain Charlotte without going into major detail? It's hard enough to dig up old memories and lay them out to be picked at. I start typing, hoping what I tell her is enough.

GEOFFREY

> Charlotte was a girlfriend years ago. She passed away.

MAGDALENA

> I'm sorry you lost her. Not to sound insensitive, but how does that tie into you calling me by her name?

I hesitate a moment. Not wanting the level of vulnerability that will come if I tell her everything. After everything I have dealt with, I can't put myself in that position again. So, I frame my words wisely.

GEOFFREY

> She was the only person I've had a relationship with. And I think the way you make me feel reminds me a little of what she and I had.

I stare at the screen, anxiously waiting for that small bubble to appear. The one that tells me she is typing a response. But the screen goes black, and my phone remains silent. Maybe she needs time to understand and process.

Mags has had me mesmerized from the beginning. Has me seeing the world differently.

She makes everything vivid. Brimming with life. Beautiful.

She managed to reignite and awaken something within me. Something I thought I'd lost long ago. The desire for knowledge. The magnificence of life. A fire that once burned bright, and extinguished alongside Charlotte. But Mags... a new flame is blazing because of her. It started as a spark—a small flicker—and has flourished into a wildfire. At times, I question if I am able to control the flames as they spread.

I ache to see her again, to mend what I have splintered. But I should dial it down a notch and let her have a chance to digest it all. Not appear desperate and always in her face. She has boundaries—parameters—and I must respect them. Give her the opportunity to adjust to us.

Not a soul could deny there is a definitive attraction between us. At times, the attraction has a life of its own, pulling us in directions we aren't ready to explore together. I'm prepared to explore every aspect of life with her. Ready to experience all the highs and lows. Smiles and tears.

But her life has history. A history I must honor and give the respect it deserves. And, after last night's blunder, it is obvious I haven't banished all the ghosts of my past either.

Mags needs things between us to grow organically. At a speed that keeps us moving forward, but doesn't launch us into the deep end too soon. However possible, I need to grant her that time. And put every ounce of effort into keeping us in a good place. I have my work cut out for me, though. Last night's slip up won't soon be forgotten.

My phone pings and I swipe open the message.

MAGDALENA

This is too important to talk about over text, but I'd like you to tell me more about her.

GEOFFREY

I haven't talked about her for a long time, but I will answer any questions you have. Are we okay?

I stare at the bouncing bubble on the screen, picking at my nails as I wait for her to respond. Why do text responses always take so fucking long?

MAGDALENA

Yes. As long as you promise to talk about it later, we're good.

I exhale, my heart settling at her words. Somehow, I will talk about Charlotte with Mags. But only when the time is right. We chat a little longer, promising to see each other on Monday.

With the weight of last night lighter on my shoulders, I kick my legs out from under the comforter, slip on a pair of lounge pants and head for the kitchen. No matter my mood, no matter how great my day starts, one truth never fails. I need coffee.

No doubt, I am currently jacked up on my new favorite drug. Mags. And although my body is pulsating from the high, coffee is a daily necessity. Something etched into my world. Something that keeps me ticking.

I turn on my single cup brewing machine and give it a moment to heat while I load the grounds. This machine is a gift from the gods. Owen gave it to me last holiday season, but there's no way I'm letting him think he is a god. No way, no how. He would have me bowing to him each day as I walked in with my cup. I couldn't give him that level of satisfaction. His ego couldn't take it, and neither could I.

The machine makes almost every type of coffee shop drink on the market, but I don't drink any of the froufrou drinks on its menu. I do, however, like my coffee strong and this machine delivers. I place my cup under the drip, press the appropriate button and let it do its thing while I grab the newspaper outside.

Sunday is always my day to sit back and relax and reset myself from everything that happened throughout the week. Weekdays didn't always provide many opportunities for downtime or relaxation, so I implemented Sunday as a "me" day. Whatever I want to do; whether it's doing absolutely nothing or hanging out with friends.

I bend and scoop up the paper sitting at the end of my driveway, scanning the front page as I walk back toward the house. Today's headline reads *Town Celebration Week Starts Tomorrow*.

Our town is turning one-hundred-years-old this week, a feat for any city to celebrate. Whispers could be heard all around town regarding rumors of what would be happening during the festivities. Countless events are scheduled each day throughout the week and into the following weekend. It is bound to be a packed week for many of the residents, as well as the business owners.

Grabbing my coffee from the brewer, I take a long draw from the steaming mug and head for the couch. I separate the front section of the paper from the pile and set the remainder on the table. I breeze over some of the town celebration topics, looking for anything eye-catching. A few pages into the front section, I spot details on the events.

I'd heard numerous activities were planned, but the town wanted to do the big reveal to all its citizens simultaneously. The only event I was privy to, prior to today's release, is the showcasing of the businesses on Thursday. And that is only because we were asked to partake as a vendor.

The town has a great line up planned. Children's crafts and games, a day for local artists, and adult crafts and hobbies. A day for restaurants to serve their favorites - food-truck-style, various food eating contests, as well as cook-offs. Small business owner's day, and the weekend is exclusive for carnival and fairground-type rides and games.

Thoughts scatter to every corner of my mind, processing all the possible things Mags and I could do during the week, and possibly into the weekend. Thrill filters through my bloodstream with a fresh dose of my new favorite drug. I can't stop myself from wanting to include her in everything.

It's automatic. And I love how it elates me.

My thoughts wander to an entirely new place, wondering if Statice will be participating in the showcase for small businesses. Could I get so lucky? I'm hopeful, but know I'm reaching for something not there.

Architectural Crimson is one of the many businesses being showcased on Thursday. It's a day where the town can flaunt its companies to the community and any visitors. The town square is slotted to hold around one hundred small-owned business booths, and the event will give us excellent exposure.

Before the doors opened for Architectural Crimson, we sat down and set parameters in place. We put hours and days into the infrastructure of our business. One thing we unanimously agreed upon, we would not take on too many projects at the same time.

This is of utmost importance to us and allows us to dedicate ourselves, and our time, to each client, giving them the individualized attention required. It also assists us in not confusing one project with the next or to feel rushed. Quality over quantity is what sets us apart from many other firms.

After turning the last page of the section, I reach for the remainder of the paper on the table. Flipping through each of the newspaper sections, I scan for anything noteworthy. When I arrive at the Local News section, the headline on the page catches my attention.

"Local Woman's Loss Years Ago Leads To Biggest Heart," I mutter to myself. Below the headline is a photo of Mags, and a couple other people I can only assume are her bosses, standing in front of the Statice Center.

My eyes lock on the image, affixed as if I'm hypnotized. She is as stunning as ever. Her dark, chocolate tresses adorning her ivory face. Her hazel eyes sparkling in the sunlight, pulling up at the corners, accentuated by her long, dark lashes. She is dressed in a cheery, pink top and a pair of black slacks, and the first thought I have is roses. Like the hint of perfume she wears.

I'm at a stalemate.

Although I know I shouldn't, I ache to read the article. The urgency to know her past, inside and out, wrenches deep in me. I want to know what happened in her life that made her so guarded. What built the wall around her heart, kept in place for so many years, giving her refuge from her feelings. To know everything about everything in her world. And to understand pieces of her that I have yet to be privy to.

But more than anything, I want to hear the words from her lips. Wanting her to be the one to want to tell me what I crave to hear.

I sit there, looking down at the newspaper article I'd placed in my lap at some point, internally burning as it took time to torment me. The black letters on the recycled gray paper blurring along with my focus.

Should I read it? After all, everything written here is now public knowledge. If she didn't want anyone to know, she wouldn't have done the interview.

Does she even know about the article? That's such a stupid question. She would have to be aware of it since she clearly posed for a photo and spoke with the writer.

Should I ask her? Maybe the journalist knew more about her past and wrote more than what they talked about during the article's interview. My head is swimming in a sea of what-ifs.

God knows I yearn to be infiltrated into this woman's world, but is this the way that I do that? Will I see her differently if I read it? Will she see me differently if she knows that I've read it?

What the hell should I do?

The paper is hot in my hands, singing thoughts into my head like some form of osmosis. A million different ideas cross my mind, but one keeps circling back around.

I don't want to get someone else's point of view about her past. It's her perspective I want. Her experiences. To hear all of it, from her lips, in her own words, with her own emotions attached. Not some edited version of her. Flat and lifeless.

Reaching for my phone, I start to message her and ask her

if she has seen the paper yet today. But I stop myself. Assured they let her know when the article would be published in the newspaper. I also don't want to disrupt the boundaries we set. I'll grant her the respect and time she needs, per her request. After all, I have a day for myself, too. Although our reasons behind having a day to ourselves are not the same, I understand her need for it.

I shift farther back onto the couch, my thought process slowly diluting right from wrong. Simmering hazels staring back at me. My eyes searching the image for the answer I know isn't going to flash on like a neon sign.

Everything circles back to the same question, over and over. *What should I do?*

My eyes drift from the image, making a beeline for the words below it. I hover over the first sentence for minutes, perhaps even hours. It read, *Meet Magdalena Bishop, the town's bravest and most compassionate woman.*

I read the sentence thirteen times. And I stop myself from going further each time I get to the last word, forcing myself to return to the first word. Temptation seeps into every ounce of my marrow, luring me with the promise of fulfillment. The fourteenth time I reach the end of the sentence, my desires get the best of me and my will caves.

I absorb every single, solitary word. Again and again.

But after I have read the article too many times to count, the high I experienced vanishes. I flip the page over, looking for a continuation. There is none.

More. I need more.

I snatch my phone, unlock it, and open the web browser. Within seconds, I am typing *Magdalena Bishop* in the Google search bar. More than one article appears, a new rush jump starting my heart. One after another, I tap the links on my screen.

As my eyes skim over every word, a sense of control slips into place. A control I lost when Charlotte was diagnosed. A control I lost when Charlotte died. I inhale deeply as relief settles in my bones and warmth spreads in my veins.

This is exactly what I needed.

CHAPTER 18

MAGDALENA

Over the last week, my and Geoff's schedules have been packed. Being busy isn't necessarily a bad thing, but it seems as if I have no time to breathe.

Geoff and I saw each other on Monday evening and last night for our Wednesday date night. Monday, I opted to have him over at my house and made dinner for us. It was wonderful to cook a meal for someone other than just myself. After Dad's stroke, he couldn't eat the same. So what and how I cooked changed.

But making a meal for Geoff and I, it was different. Different from dinners with Dad. Different from dinners with Lessa and Lena.

Special.

Fulfilling in a new way. It gave me a sense of purpose and joy. Not that I was some kitchen wizard, but I did love trying new things.

And this was a unique way to share a part of me with him.

And I wanted to share more of myself with him. As long as

We chatted over dinner, talking about our days apart and anything new we had going on at work. A few times, I caught Geoff fidgeting out the corner of my eye. Maybe it was the whole Charlotte thing making him antsy.

I gave him plenty of opportunities to bring her up, but he never did. And it irked me a little. He promised me we would talk about her. So why hasn't he brought it up?

Last night, we checked out the town's festivities for our date. The weeknights weren't as inundated, but there was still plenty to see and do. We strolled around the town square, hand-in-hand, and tasted numerous samples from area restaurants and food trucks.

After dinner, we watched an eating contest—people attempting to eat a hundred hot wings the quickest. First of all —who on earth would want to eat that much food? Second— how did they not get sick from it?

Until witnessing the actual event, I never realized how entertaining it could be to watch such a thing. It was intriguing, to say the least. But also disgusting and addicting.

We sat in the sea of collapsible, plastic chairs and cheered for random contestants. We called them *red shirt guy* or *green shirt lady*. After the *blue shirt guy* won, we gave him a high five on his victory. He proudly wore his first place ribbon and snapped photos with anyone who asked.

While we strolled through the square, we discussed going to the Lake Lavender Centennial Festival on Saturday. It wasn't something the town did regularly, so it would be a great memory to share with Geoff. Laughter, rides, and tons of fun.

But with all the conversations we had during our date nights, never once did Geoff mention Charlotte. It should be him who brings her up, not me. Time after time, I left openings. Hinted at things I thought would stir up such a conversation. But it never came. And part of me thinks it never will.

Why won't he bring it up? Why do I have a feeling it will be me who does?

Once I have a minute to breathe at Statice, I send Geoff a quick message.

MAGDALENA

> I had a great time last night. Counting down till Saturday.

Now, my phone sits like a hot pan on my bare hands. My eyes unwilling to leave the screen as I reread the message I sent him.

Who am I? And what have I done with the old me? Two questions that have me pondering if I'm the same woman from a week ago. It frightens me in both a good and bad way. I'm not quite sure if I recognize who I am when we're together. As if I have an alter ego who has been under lock and key for the last several years.

Yes, the message I sent him is simple. All I told him was that I had a great time last night and couldn't wait for Saturday. To most people, that wouldn't seem such a horrible notion. But I'm not most people. Waiting for his response has me jittery.

And Charlotte kept niggling in the back of my mind. Aside from being Geoff's girlfriend, who was she? What happened with her to make Geoff stop dating? It had to have been awful.

Deep breath in, deep breath out. He will tell me when he's ready. This much I believe.

Aside from the Charlotte moment, Geoff has brought a part of me back to life. He doesn't tiptoe around me or make me feel fragile. He treats me like a woman, not a pity case. It is refreshing and makes me feel as if I can breathe for the first time in years. The spiked thrum of my heart when he's near is a testament to the excitement he sparks.

But when he touches me.

Every touch, every caress, shoots heat across every inch of my body and stirs at my core.

Just thinking about him right now… My insides ignite like the Fourth of July. My thoughts exploding with what could be. My body coming to life—blossoming, expanding, exploring. This is what he's done for me.

Awakened my soul. Brought possibility back into my world.

My phone pings with a response from Geoff.

GEOFFREY

Hey Mags! I had a great time too! Looking forward to Saturday x

MAGDALENA

How's the booth going? I think everyone must be there.

GEOFFREY

Actually, a little slow for me. Other booths are non-stop. One potential client. That's good.

MAGDALENA

Not too many people looking for an architect, huh? At least it's almost over.

GEOFFREY

Yeah, I think more people are interested in the hairstylist and retail shops.

MAGDALENA

I'm sure. I'll let you get back to the fun ;) Talk to you later x

I set my phone down like it is the most fragile thing I own. I'm giddy like a schoolgirl over her guy. I can't stop the silly, fun-loving feelings he gives me. The urge to share my high school girl feelings with Lessa and Lena spins inside me. 'Cause that's what girls do, right? Share with their girlfriends.

I wish tonight was girl's night. I know the three of us all have things going on already, even if they aren't out and about plans. I use my evenings alone to decompress and center myself after being at Statice. I'm sure Lessa and Lena do something similar since they run their own businesses.

It isn't as if my mind or body always demanded downtime each day after work, but some days dredge up a lot of memories and emotions. Reliving some of the worst days of my life is not a simple feat and it's best to have the capability of releasing what comes.

Thankfully, I've had many teachers over the years who each taught me various coping mechanisms. All the love and support and sleepless nights made me stronger. They gave me the ability to pass along my strength to others, at their darkest time. And for that, I am beyond grateful.

Lessa and Lena are the most significant contributors to my recovery. I owe them everything. I know they would dive into the deep end and do it all over again in a heartbeat, as I would for them. But a newfound sensation lingers inside me. A new warmth coating my heart. And this radiating warmth soothes me, coaxes me to believe I'll never need anyone in that capacity again. Because this feeling, the one that flickers and burns and grows more radiant inside of me, tells me I'm strong enough to handle whatever life throws my way.

I shake my head, wiping away the temporary layer of melancholy and replacing it with bliss and affection. I snap back into my delightful state of hair twirling and body fidgeting. I cannot wait until tomorrow to talk to them. The bonds of sisterhood scream inside me, the inkling to share my excitement with the world is palpable.

I pick up my phone again, scrolling through my previous messages and tap on the group chat between the three of us. How to begin? They'll be elated, knowing I'm putting myself out into the world more. But how do I broach the topic?

My fingers scroll over the screen, clicking letters and forming a straightforward thought.

MAGDALENA

The sheltered girl has come out to play...

My finger hovers over the send button for a moment as I read the words aloud to myself. *I can do this. I am not afraid. Just be yourself.*

I hit send.

Within seconds, I have messages from both of them blowing up my phone. My inner teenager jumping up and down in jubilant hysterics.

WELCOME
to
LAKE LAVENDER

I rummage through my closet for the umpteenth time within the last hour. It has never taken so much effort for me to find something to wear. I swear I have yanked every shirt off its hanger, trying to pair something with the jeans I have chosen. Never in my life has the act of dressing myself been such a challenge.

I peer over at the mountain of shirts on my bed, inadequacy rising inside me for the first time in my life. I don't own a sufficient wardrobe for dating and I am half tempted to call for back up. Somehow, I manage to locate my phone, buried under *Mount-Killing-Me-With-Cotton*. With rapid-fire fingers, I type a message out to Lessa and Lena, indicating I am in freak out mode. But my fingers pause over the keyboard on my screen, and I stop myself.

I shouldn't always run to them every time I can't figure out what to wear on a date. Of course, they would stop whatever they're doing in a heartbeat and chime in with advice. Or possibly come over and help me. But I need to step up and learn how to be this newer version of myself. Yes, they would be here to help me with anything. As would I for them. But I should take this step on my own. Go through the motions and experience the moments I missed out on when I was younger.

Although it is normal to some, dating is a huge change for me. And dating Geoff is different than the previous guys I'd spent time with. None of them panned out. The guys were just... blah. There were no sparks. No butterflies. No desire or ache or longing to see them again. And I going to my mom to ask questions wasn't an option. Sure, I had Beatrice, but she was busy at the center. At times, it felt burdensome to ask Beatrice things about boys and relationships. She was busy with so many other kids and I didn't want to bog her down any further. Dad was willing to talk about boys and relationships with me, but it wasn't the same. He meant well, but it was odd talking about those kinds of feelings with him. And embarrassing to some degree.

After Dad's stroke, dating shifted to the back burner. Practically his at-home nurse for close to three years and also attending college online, there was really no time. Guys and relationships were the furthest priority in my life. And I was okay with that. Because Dad needed me more than anyone else.

But that was then.

And now, I am learning to live again. Feeling many of the emotions I missed out on for several years. In some respects, I have been catching up on almost a decade's worth of experiences. And some days are more overwhelming than others.

Geoff intrigues me, though. He sparks something inside me. Has cracked the barrier around my heart, removing the bricks one-by-one. From the beginning with him, we had the potential to be more, in every capacity.

So why do I resist taking things further? After the first date and his attention to my body, God knows I'm hungry for more. But as much as my body craves more from him physically, a small part of me hesitates. Is it the whole Charlotte talk we haven't had?

Shaking off my thoughts, I focus on getting ready for tonight's date. I walk back to my closet and ogle over the tops hanging there. Honestly, it doesn't matter what shirt I choose. They all pair well with my jeans. And he'll like whatever I wear. So, I change my mindset and look at everything as if I were going out for girl's night. Simple. Easy.

My fingers run over the array of colors and stop on a soft blue, long sleeve Henley. The tone elicits a vision of his eyes. Eyes that swallow me into their depths for days.

Tugging on the sleeve, the shirt slips off the hanger and into my hands. Before exiting my closet, I also grab my denim jacket. Since we'll be outside, and the fall weather is beginning to descend onto the town, I'd rather have it than not.

I wiggle the shirt over my head and then check my appearance in the mirror. Perfect. The concept of not being able to find the perfect top suddenly seems less of a big deal.

I snatch the pile of shirts adorning my bed and take them back to the closet, hanging them in their place. I'm not a huge fan of clutter or disorganization. Some might go as far as to call me a bit of a neat-freak. But I just like everything in its place.

Reaching down, I snag a pair of sneakers and socks. I'm not sure if we are eating at the festival or somewhere beforehand, but we will be wandering around a while tonight. With all the games and rides, we're likely to be there for hours.

I check the time on my way to the living room, the large hands pointedly displaying twelve after five. Less than twenty minutes until Geoff arrives. And like clockwork, my nerves spark to life. He's nowhere near me and I'm already a little woozy, my stomach in knots. Will it always be like this? A small part of me hopes so.

I switch into rush mode. I bolt for the bathroom, checking my hair to see if any strands are out of place and touching up the little bit of makeup I'd put on. And after spritzing a small amount of perfume on my neck, I'm officially ready.

Heading back to the living room, my eyes scan for anything out of place or in need of clean up. Whenever I am antsy, and at home, I become a cleaning machine. It busies my mind and distracts me, only in the slightest, from whatever has me on edge.

Moments later, I hear a knock at the door. *Geoff. He's here!*

Drawing on every tranquil-filled molecule inside me, I walk to the front door, taking a deep breath before turning the handle. The door swings open, slower than usual, and, inch by inch, Geoff comes into view.

Holy hell. I don't know what it is, but this man does things to my body. Every chemical within me stirs. Every millimeter of my flesh vibrates with desire for him. Every molecule in my body aches for him.

"Hey…" The only word I can manage rolls off my tongue with a low rasp.

"Hey. You ready to go?"

He can read me like a book. My body and voice hide nothing from him. And I'm not entirely sure I want to shelter any of it from him. If anything, I want to expose more of myself to him.

"Let me just grab my purse."

Purse in hand, I head to the door, locking it behind me as I step out on the patio. He reaches for my hand, surprising me, bringing it to his mouth and kissing my knuckles with a soft brush of his lips.

With such a simple gesture, I stand speechless as the fluttering behind my ribcage magnifies. I am in so much deeper than I thought. And I'm still unsure if that's a good thing.

He drives us to the central part of town, where the festivities are occurring. The trip quiet, and the silence between us not as comfortable as it has been in the past. Part of me itches to ask him more about Charlotte. Or maybe his family. He hasn't mentioned anyone other than his two guy friends—not that I have spilled my life to him.

"Was that okay?"

I'm not sure what he's referring to, and the confusion must show on my face.

"Kissing you. Was that okay?"

"Most definitely it was okay." *Did that come off sounding desperate?*

"I'm glad. I was worried by your silence."

"No need to worry. I was just thinking about how I'd like to know more about you."

His jaw goes taut. A few seconds later, he gnashes his teeth. It almost feels as if he refuses to look my way. Is he upset with me? Because I want to know him? "There's not much to tell," he clips.

His sudden switch in behavior has me jerking back in my seat an inch. Right now, Geoff is someone else. "How can that be true?" I mumble, trying to lighten the sudden heaviness. "No one becomes who they are without a little history behind it."

His eyes leave the road for a beat, glancing at me. The way his eyes pinch tight has me sinking further into the seat. "True. How about this," he suggests. "Let's enjoy the festival tonight. After, we can talk more. Alright?"

I didn't want the evening bogged down with the sad stories of our past, so I agree. After the idea simmers down, he reaches across the seat and takes my hand. And for a beat, I wonder if he's touching me to placate what he has agreed to.

His thumbs paint small circles on my skin, easing the slight tension from a moment ago. He will talk when he's ready. I just need to give him more time. And patience.

"Mags, I'm sorry I snapped at you. The effect you have on me... It's difficult to talk about my past. I'm sure you understand." His tone sympathetic as he continues the soothing strokes on my palm.

I do understand. But how would he know that? We haven't discussed my parents. How would he guess I, too, have a difficult past? "Yeah, I get it," I say, confused.

The remaining drive to the festival is laden with a heavy silence looming over us. Each of us venturing deeper and getting lost in our own heads. Emotions I'm eager to express are purposely shoved aside to keep myself guarded and safe from experiencing pain. And I hate the fact that I'm suppressing myself.

The strained distance between us, despite our mutual attraction, has me on alert. But I can't deny my heart. I can't deny the exhilaration when he is near.

I can't fight reality. Or what he does to me.

Brick by brick, I'm tearing down that wall. I'm letting him inside.

And how I hunger to let him in.

To allow him to know me.

Every aspect of me.

"Mags..." he whispers, startling me. "You've awakened something inside me. And sometimes it scares me, how strongly I feel about you. Because it's new and has happened so fast. And I don't want to mess this up."

His admission plucks at my heartstrings. Things between us have evolved quickly. Does it scare me? Absolutely. Would I change any of it? Never. "That's not fair. Anything I say after that will seem inconsequential."

"Just say what's on your mind. It's a little early in our relationship to be so deep, but... I believe in honesty."

I muster up the courage to respond. I haven't shared the hidden parts of myself in years. But every fiber in me longs to share with Geoff. It's not fair for either of us to be in the dark. "Before you got to my house tonight, I was a wreck. Fumbling over what to wear and my appearance. Two things I never do." I pause, collecting my thoughts. "I busied myself with menial tasks to pass the time. But the moment you knocked on my door... My nervousness vanished. I don't understand it, and *that* scares me."

The tables turn and he is unresponsive. A small hurricane spins in my gut. But for too many years, I sat silent. Never expressing my emotions. Scared of what would happen if I did. I no longer wanted to suppress my heart.

"Mags... we will continue to surprise each other. But please remember, we're doing this at your pace. When you're ready. For whatever. I will be here."

"Thank you." It's all I say, although a voice inside me begs to hear more. Why is it I share these little pieces of myself and he doesn't reciprocate? My telling him I am scared of my feelings for him... Isn't that an open invitation for him to say more? To respond with something other than our relationship going at my pace?

I respect that he allows me to take the lead. But is it enough? Relationships are a partnership. Each of us should give and take equally. So why does it feel like I'm the only one giving? And he only takes?

Not wanting to ruin what should be a fun evening, I shove the thoughts to the back of my mind. Not forgotten, just stashed away for a later time. Because it's a conversation we need to have—soon.

A moment later, the lights, sounds, and smells rush in around us. The streets are lined with people walking from the parking area to the festivities. Everyone's jubilation dancing in the cooler night air. Kids yank their parents' hands, excited to ride the rides and eat all the greasy, sugary food. Adults line up for games like they're ten-plus years younger.

Geoff parks the car and feeds the meter. The energy flowing through the air from the event is exhilarating. Like many of the children I see along the street, I want to grab

Geoff's hand and draw him toward the entrance. But he beats me to it.

I laugh at the adolescent nature in which we are behaving. I love it and don't want it to end.

"I hope you don't mind, but I thought we could eat here. We don't get such treats often and I thought it would be fun." His smile erases the worry I had minutes ago, replacing it with elation. And with that simple curve of his lips, I am young and carefree.

The scent of battered foods being fried fills my nose, my mouth instantly salivating. "I'm in. Let's go scope out the food vendors first, if that's okay with you?"

"Definitely. Then we can decide if we want to eat before we ride anything."

We wander around the festival, scanning the rides and games as we head in the direction of all the food. I know we're at least a good football field away, but the smell of pure deliciousness populates the air, and I am eager to discover all the heavenly options we have to choose from.

"Oh my god! Can you smell that? I think we just arrived in carnival food heaven."

Laughter erupts from him like I have told the funniest joke known to man. It is a genuine laugh. Not forced. Not on for show. And it plucks at my insides yet again, opening foreign feelings that are becoming more and more welcome.

"Are you laughing at me?" I tease.

"You can't tell me that wasn't funny? Did you hear yourself? If that were me, you'd be laughing too, and you know it."

And his words make me join in on the laughter. Only he can make me laugh at myself and be okay with it.

We end up grabbing food from several vendors to share— fried mac and cheese bites, mini corn dogs, hand nachos, and some kind of donut burger. If one thing is certain, it's the fact that I am leaving here tonight a few pounds heavier, and it is going to be great.

We demolish the mountain of delight in no time flat. No words can describe my current food high. It's this crazy, buzzy sensation floating around my heart, pumping through my veins, and pricking my skin. Geoff tells me he's on the same journey and suggests maybe we walk around a bit before we ride anything. I agree without hesitation.

Along the way, we play different games and win cute prizes—a stuffed animal and a goldfish, which I give to the kids playing beside us. After our stomachs settle a bit, we ride a few of the rides, starting with the tame Ferris wheel. One thing that's great about the Ferris wheel—we stop at the top and sit under the stars while people fill the cars, my eyes never leaving the sky.

It is all so wonderful, and yet something feels off.

Is it because he has yet to explain Charlotte? Or how he assumed I understood discussing the past was difficult? That one still has me curious.

"Geoff," I whisper, shifting my eyes from the stars to his. "Can you tell me about Charlotte?"

He clenches his jaw, his vibrant eyes lock on mine. Relaxing his jaw, he says, "I already told you a little about her. Don't you think it's time you tell me about you?"

His evasion has me second-guessing whether or not I should've started the conversation. But I want us to be able to talk about this. His past, and mine.

"How about this," I suggest. "I share something and then you tell me more. Deal?"

The cogs spin, his eyes darting between mine. He wants to

accept the offer, but something holds him back. *What could be so bad to have him hesitant?*

The Ferris wheel starts back up, the car wobbling us. But his eyes hold mine. He's on the verge.

"Okay. Deal," he cedes. "But you first."

I nod, huffing. *Just be yourself.*

I inhale deep, rambling soft on my exhale. "When I was sixteen, my mom passed away. It was sudden. But losing her was grueling for my dad and me. It took a long time to accept it. Sometimes, I wonder if I really have."

Geoff's expression softens, but something in his eyes has me perplexed. Or rather, the lack of something. There's no surprise. Like what I told him isn't new information. But I haven't shared this with him before. "I'm sorry about your mom, Mags. What was she like?"

"She was the most amazing woman I've ever known. Kind. Gentle. Selfless. And she put her heart into everything that mattered." A lone tear rolls down my cheek, Geoff's thumb swiping it away.

"Don't cry," he whispers, leaning in. His lips inches from mine. "She sounds as wonderful as you."

"I wish that were true."

"It is." He closes the gap between us, brushing his lips against mine. And for a moment, under the stars, I'm lost in his kiss.

When we break apart, I weave my fingers with his. "What was Charlotte like?"

The Ferris wheel car stops at the bottom and we hop out. We walk hand-in-hand before sitting on a bench away from the foot traffic.

He closes his eyes, his hand trembling in mine. I clutch his hand, hoping to give him the reassurance he needs.

He drags in a breath, his eyes opening. A sadness sits there, an unhealed wound. "Charlotte and I dated most of high school. Our relationship was serious. We had mapped out our entire future... together." He pauses, tipping his head to the night sky. "She visited the doctor because of a pain in her abdomen. After several tests, she was diagnosed with stage four ovarian cancer. It metastasized and was affecting her uterus."

Silence consumes me. There is nothing I can say to make this better. If he was anything like me, he didn't want to hear apologies. He didn't want pity. He just wanted to move forward.

But how can he move forward if he doesn't talk about Charlotte more and what happened to her? And what happened to him because of her. Yes, he gave me a glimpse into their past. But it still feels like he's evading. There has to be more to the story if he swore off relationships after her.

He gives my hand a gentle squeeze. "Want to grab dessert and head out?"

Bringing my gaze level with his, I study his expression. An odd desperation swims in his eyes, begging me to not ask anything else now. We will continue this conversation, but just not now. "Yeah. I'd like that."

We stop and share a giant funnel cake and a deep-fried candy bar. There really is no comparison in the world of sweets. Carnival foods in a realm all their own. I wish that realm was around more often.

The drive back is solemn. Neither of us speaks, but our hands stay connected.

As his car turns onto my street, the air in the car thickens. So much has come to light tonight.

But something nags at me. *Something still feels off.*

As honest and open as we have been all night, it feels like there's still more hidden away. But maybe the best thing to do is let Geoff tell me in his own time. I may have been ready to open up to him, but losing first loves and losing parents are two totally different things. He will tell me when he's ready. And me? I just need to be patient and give him the time to do so.

He cuts the engine and we sit in my driveway, our thoughts racing separate paths. Mine is running a marathon. And I decide to not press him further tonight. But I know I'm missing something.

He reaches for the door and, with reluctance, gets out and makes his way to my door. His stride is unhurried, his demeanor unreadable. I slide out of my seat and walk up the path to my front door with him beside me, my fingers lacing with his.

I unlock the door and stare at the handle clutched in my hand. His breath is on my neck, chills racing down my spine. I shiver, but otherwise don't move. His hand creeps up my left arm and then down the side of my torso toward my waist.

Invite him in tonight.

"Mags." His voice loaded and wanton.

I spin to face him; his piercing blues cause me to stumble back. They're brilliantly blue and boring into the epicenter of my soul. Focusing on my lips, he starts closing the gap between us, waiting to see if I'll stop him.

I don't.

I want to kiss him again.

I want him against me.

His lips hover over mine, caressing me with his breath. We stand like this for several panting breaths. Closing his eyes, he takes my mouth with his. Warm, supple, and greedy for me, but still gentle.

Heat simmers in my core and I wrap my arms around his center, drawing him closer to me. His hands stroke the sides of my face, holding and guiding me along the path of his delicious assault. It is euphoric, and I want to take what's happening between us inside, away from any prying eyes.

I reach behind me, twisting the doorknob and pushing the door open. Without notice, his lips aren't on mine anymore, my mouth suddenly bereft. His eyes probe mine with the question of what will happen next.

I lean forward, placing a small, slow kiss on his lips. As I pull away, I wrap his hand in mine and walk him into the foyer, closing the rest of the world away from us.

CHAPTER 19

MAGDALENA

"Are you sure?"

"I don't think I've ever been more sure about anything." He needs my assurance and acceptance. That I want us, here and now.

Our hands still laced, I tug him closer. When he's this close, it's intoxicating. Crystalline eyes dilated. Sweet teakwood tickling my nose. Skin heated under my touch. It jump starts my heart and drives my hunger.

Our lips meet again, scorching me. I'm ravenous and feral, and cannot get enough of him. As if my thoughts are broadcasted, he deepens the kiss and lures me in further. Our tongues dipping and sliding, caressing and memorizing.

My hands shift to rest on his shoulders. My thumbs tuck under the edges of his jacket and clutch the lapels. His hands trace along the curves of my hips—his grip causing me to gasp —crushing me flush against his body.

His desire undeniable for me. Our insatiable arousal encasing us in our own little bubble. Our lips shift from desire

I slide his jacket off his shoulders, letting it fall to the floor.

His hands trail into the opening of my denim jacket, slipping under and pushing it off my body. His palms frame my face, tracing my jawline and tugging my loose tendrils. A deep-seated need for him flourishes inside me. "God, I want you," I groan, his fingers clenching my biceps.

Gracefully, I walk backward and lead us toward my bedroom. Our pace slow. My back bumps against the door and I kick it open and lead us in.

The back of my knees hits the mattress, our bodies motionless. His thumbs paint gentle strokes over my cheeks as he paints slow, tender kisses on my lips. He backs away with hesitance and adds a few inches between us.

He searches my face, checking my assurance remains intact. His eyes smolder—a crystalline rimmed with the deepest shade of blue—and captivate me. Craving his lips, I lean forward. But he pulls back in equal measure.

Why is he doing that? My eyes tighten as I watch him. "Did I do something wrong?"

He shakes his head, slow and intentional. "No, Mags. The complete opposite, actually. I just want you to be sure that this is what you want. What I feel for you... This will take those feelings to a whole new level. I need to know you're sure. You and me... it's not just some tryst."

His words roll around in my head. As fogged with lust as I am, I process what he says. He doesn't want to hurt me. He doesn't want me to hurt him. Neither had crossed my mind nor did I want them to. I would never intentionally hurt someone in that way, especially myself.

"Yes. I'm sure."

The muscles in his face and body relax as he studies me. He

takes the trust I give him and stashes it in a safe place. His eyes close as he stands unmoving a moment.

His hands graze my hips again and settle there, giving my shirt hem a slight tug. I'm lost as I survey his face, mesmerized by the small expressions flitting across it. I run my hands slowly up his chest, stopping when I reach his face, thumbs resting on his chin and lips.

Lips parting the smallest degree, his chest expands, coming in rapid bursts. Seconds later, a pair of lust drunk blue eyes meet mine, and they're saying all the right things to my body.

His lips crush mine with renewed passion. This is more—deeper, all-consuming. Our kissing from the front door to the bedroom comparable to child's play now.

And I hunger for more.

My shirt hem in his loose fists, he drags it up my torso, pacing himself enough to drive me insane. My hands and lips drop from his face long enough for my shirt to be hoisted over my head and slide down my arms.

His fingers ghost down my spine, eliciting a shiver. Warm lips break from mine and graze my jawline, nipping their way to my ear and suckling my lobe, my body arching into him, aching for his touch. His hands scrape along my hips, kneading a path around my waist, his mouth worshiping the cusp of my throat, each nip of his teeth driving my need for him higher.

He is everywhere. His lips and tongue and touch. Sensations soar and ignite under each nip and lick and taste of my skin. Fire scorches every fiber and cell inside me. It is everything.

Warm hands dance their sweet ascent again, trickling their way up my spine and pausing at my bra. A slight pop fills the air before the straps slip off my shoulders. My bra still in his hands, my breasts remain concealed behind the thin material.

His lips edge their way back up to mine, kissing me deep. When he draws back, I open my eyes and am pinned with the piercing force emanating from his hooded blues. My heart pounds wild under my ribcage, the pulsing organ so loud Geoff could probably hear it. His eyes lock on mine as he lets go of my bra, my buds peaking when the air hits them.

A tingle spreads across my skin as he nips my chin, lips walking down the front of my throat and sending my face skyward, gasping. His knuckles skim my stomach and pause under my breasts, my body trembling in their wake. The tips of his hair tickle my skin as his head dips lower, meeting where his thumbs stroke my nipples.

Small pecks and nibbles graze the flesh below my collarbones, and I arch into his touch. One hand shifts, skimming along my torso until it meets the small of my back, and gives way to the heat of his mouth. His lips wrap around the stiff peak, his teeth tugging, an electric, white heat igniting and delving straight into my core.

"Oh fuck," I hiss.

My breath heaves in quick, audible bursts. My fingers weave into the soft threads of his hair, curling into loose fists, drawing his mouth back to mine. My need for him is unhealthy, but I won't let that stop my desperation. He is everything I longed for, and I yearn to absorb every particle of him into me.

My hands trace the lines of his back, yanking at his shirt's hem and tugging up, urgent to remove the barrier. His muscular torso on display, I outline his definition before gravitating closer. The length of his body hot against mine. My desire intensifies. Fingers skimming along his naked flesh does potent things to me—a deep throb curling in my core.

His fingers tempt and tease my body. A tide of charged energy left in its wake, pulsating. He cups my face, magnetizing our lips, and lowers me onto the bed. A soft thump echoes in the room—his shoes kicked off and I mimic his action.

The bed dips, the mattress shifting under his weight as we come face-to-face. I study the sharp edge of his jaw, noticing the way his hair falls on either side of his face as he hovers above me, how he focuses his eyes on my lips.

The sheer beauty of this man stuns me silent. Not just his physical allure, but also how attentive and gentle and devoted he is. A rush of emotions swirl inside me, puncturing my chest, the sensations foreign and beguiling. A dose of pleasure and pain.

His fingers trace my cheek, gaze still locked. "You're so beautiful," he whispers.

I lose all sense as he kisses down my midline, stopping above my waistline. He feathers kisses around my navel, his hands trailing up my sides. My back arches off the bed, my body craving his tongue everywhere.

Lips crawling up my stomach, leaving bites in their wake, and stopping when they hit the peaks of my breast, tending to them one by one. My nails claw the comforter, digging and kneading as he consumes me.

There's a tug at my jeans and a new shot of adrenaline injects into my bloodstream. Unclenching my fists, my hands trace his shoulders and upper back before I sink my nails in and drag them up until they weave in his hair. With a firm grip, I lift his head and bring his line of sight to mine. What I see in his eyes...

Passion.

Hunger.

Intoxication.

And I lose myself in him.

Our lips meet again before he moves away—kissing, sucking and biting his way back to my navel—and finishes unzipping my jeans. The mattress shifts and his weight leaves the bed, a burst of cold air prickling goose-flesh across my skin. His fingers hook the waist of my jeans, dragging them down and depositing them on the floor. Heavy breathing fills the room. The teeth of his zipper separate, his jeans joining mine on the floor. The bed dips, his hands pressing on the bed.

And then he is *there*.

At the molten core of my desire, grinding his chin over the lace of my panties.

Inhaling the pheromones coaxing him in. A thick, throaty growl escapes his chest, flaming the fire within me further. His hands beside my knees, he slowly glides up and stops at my panties.

With a seamless shift, my panties drift down my legs. And for a brief moment of time, we're just there. His body adorning mine. The only thing between us is his boxer briefs.

Moonlight casts away some of the darkness blanketing us, and I notice his eyes closed above mine. *He needs a moment.*

This isn't meaningless for either of us, and the impact must be stronger for him than I initially thought. Without a second thought, I frame his face, stroking his cheeks. And wait for him to open his eyes and see me.

For me to see what he is thinking, and he I.

And then he opens them, and they glow so beautiful in the moonlit room. He steals my breath—literally. As hurried as we were to get to this point, time has become an anomaly, slowing down and pacing every move we make. He lowers his lips to mine, kissing me tenderly and without words, asking me one last time for permission.

Our mouths continue their tender exchange, my hands skirting down to his waist and clutching his underwear. He breaks our kiss, his blues on my hazels. "Yes," I breathe.

I want him.

All of him.

Without hesitation.

He assists my hands at removing his briefs.

Fever spreads over my entirety as his body contacts mine. My hands discover his muscular upper traps, cascading their way down and taking in his defined frame and landing on the firmness of his gluts. His body divine, and it's unfathomable he belongs to me.

Our mouths and hands explore, driving the intensity higher and higher. He repositions and settles his erection against my core. Without hesitation, I drive forward into his pressure, reiterating my ache for more.

He grabs my wrists with his hands and pushes them toward the headboard. One hand pins mine while the other descends down the curves of my body, stopping at the base of my buttock. His body shifts as his lips leave mine.

Opening my eyes, I glimpse the expression flitting his face, and my breath hitches. His features express a hundred emotions and I don't think it's possible to transcribe them all. Desire. Longing. Desperation. And something else. Something much deeper.

My lips part, my back bowing off the bed as his length enters me. I forget how to breathe. How to blink or speak. All cognition vanishes. He stills—watching me, waiting for me to let him know I'm okay. That he hasn't hurt me.

Removing my hands from his grip, I frame his face, taking his bottom lip between my lips and sucking softly while lifting my hips and pushing him further inside me. "Oh, god. Don't stop, Geoff."

Absolute. Utter. Euphoria.

It's as if my body is an instrument only he knows how to play. Hitting every note. Striking every chord. Creating a symphony between us. Sweet, tantalizing, unadulterated bliss.

Our bodies synchronize into a delicious rhythm, measured and unabashed. My hands glide down his spine, caressing the fevered sheen, and halting on his backside. I sink my nails into him and force him deeper into me on his next thrust forward.

"Jesus, Mags," he grunts.

No amount of what he gives is enough. More. I want more. I've never needed another person like I do him. It's an all-consuming desperation. Complete fulfillment. It is both thrilling and terrifying.

I drag my nails up his back—his flesh marring in my wake —and sink my fingers in his hair, yanking with force. The motion evokes a loud hiss from his lips, his pace becoming more vigorous and frenzied. He tips his head forward, our foreheads touching. Harsh breaths hover in the air and drive the inferno in my core to new heights.

A new sensation builds within me. Overriding everything else I know. Urging me onward. Flipping a switch inside and taking hold of every rational part of me. Driving me to an unknown plateau of ecstasy.

The pitch in my sounds change, followed by the guttural moans emanating from his chest. At the precipice of his rapture. Somewhere I had never been. Somewhere I never want to leave.

Stars float in my vision as my body ignites from my climax.

It robs me of all my senses, drawing me into a heavenly abyss. Holding me in a place I have no desire to leave.

His lips crush mine, his thrusts hasten. Although my orgasm tapered, I urge his hungry possession of me. An intense, throaty moan reverberates from his core and into me, driving me wild. Pushing me further.

Intensity grows in the deepest parts of me and is mystifying and irresistible. I yearn to live in this feeling with him. Endlessly. His breathing quickens. His sounds intensify. Compelling me to ascend this peak with him. Our breaths synchronizing. Our lips molded into one. Our movements in complete symmetry.

An eruption detonates from my core once more, sending him over the edge and tumbling into the sweet, sweet abyss with me.

CHAPTER 20

GEOFFREY

My desk is drowning in paperwork. Our firm has never been this busy. And it's phenomenal.

Mid-phase on a new project, building drawings and specs cover every inch of my desk space. I love bringing new projects to life. Seeing another entrepreneur's dream erect in our town.

Lake Lavender was a notch above small-town status. Main Street ran two miles down the center of town, lined with brick-walled storefronts, windows painted with images and phrases to advertise products, and lampposts every fifteen feet. Wide sidewalks laid between the shops and street parking. Various large evergreens planted between every other store. At the center of Main Street was a park. It spanned both sides of the road and was a block wide. On beautiful weather days, children laughed and ran around the playground. Adults walked the trails or sat on benches and enjoyed the scenery.

One of the best parts of Lake Lavender was the individuality. Franchised or chain businesses were accessible, but sat on the outskirts of town. The town prided itself on small businesses and its owners. And it was one of the most attractive qualities Lake Lavender possessed.

Our current project would bring new life to a current restaurant. They have outgrown their patronage and we were developing their expansion. New outdoor seating with a view of the park on Main Street. The same section of park Mags and I strolled through a few weeks back.

I organize the plans and drawings, placing them back in their folder and tube storage. Checking my calendar, I scan next week's schedule before heading out. Just as packed with meetings and planning as this week.

Logan pops his head in. "You done for the day?"

"Yeah, man," I say as I drop my keys and wallet in my pockets, my eyes avert from his.

He's quiet and the intensity of his stare drills holes in me. "So, things good with you? And that woman?"

After snatching my suit jacket from the desk chair, I regard him. "Things are spectacular. Thanks," I beam.

Logan's expression relaxes a smidge. "Glad to hear. Have a good night, man." He waves me off and walks away.

In fact, the last few weeks have been unimaginable. Mags and I inseparable, except for work. Our time together has doubled, her boundaries fading away. She is opening her world to me. Allowing me to see how life can go from mono-chromatic to prismatic.

The morning after we'd had sex, there was zero awkward-ness. Ebbing and flowing around each other as if we had done it hundreds of times. It was so natural. So perfect.

And since that night, we've spent our weekends glued at the hip. Two weekends back, she asked me to stay at her place. I didn't take the gesture lightly. It was a level of trust I secured close to my heart. It was both thrilling and frightening.

Until she wanted to stay at my house last weekend. No woman has stayed in my bed. Even with the various distractions I've had over the years, not a single woman stepped foot inside my home. It was a rule I'd implemented to ease future complications.

But Mags in my house. In my space. It was paradise. I never wanted her to leave. She is my oxygen. The blood pumping through my veins. The reason I sought more for the first time since Charlotte.

Things at Statice have tapered off for Mags, and she was thankful. For a while, she felt impeded by the lack of volunteers. But in the last week, two new volunteers came on, and it has been an immense help for everyone. Her relief evident, her body relaxing more with each passing day. And what a difference it made for us.

"That was fantastic," I say as I pat my stomach.

"Easy peasy. I'm sure anyone could've made it."

Sometimes it boggles my mind how easily Mags dismisses compliments. I love that she isn't as vain as many women. But I wish she would learn to accept compliments—small or large.

After devouring Mags' delicious cooking, we cocoon ourselves in a blanket and scan the television for something to watch.

"Anything you want to watch?" I ask.

She shakes her head and snuggles closer to me, tucking her chin into the crook of my neck. I bask in the way her body molds against mine. Every dip and curve and line between us comes together like lost puzzle pieces. A perfect fit.

We choose a romantic comedy neither of us has seen. The laughter balancing out the romance just enough.

The next two hours flood with laughter, a couple of times into tears, and teasing one another. Nights like this, everything fades away. Nothing more important than the woman curled into my side, her arms wrapped around my waist. Being with Mags makes me feel human again. She radiates possibility and new beginnings and love.

Often, I daydream of our future together. And I picture every aspect of my future including her. I envision us living together and how astounding it would be to lay next to her every day and night. To blend our worlds together, to talk about work and friends and anything.

I foresee us being together forever. Images flash in my mind of me sliding a ring onto her fourth finger, the only one with a vein leading straight to her heart. My heart starts racing, and I hope she can't feel it.

But every time ideas of the future stir inside me, I remember having those same thoughts about Charlotte and me. How we planned to get married after high school and have children when we hit thirty. And then I remember how she was stolen from me.

And when I glance over at Mags out of the corner of my eye, pain wrenches my heart and steals my breath. I care about her so much. Too much. And my biggest fear is losing her too. Not necessarily in the same way I lost Charlotte, but losing her in any way. I would be devastated.

Part of me knows I need to talk to her more about Charlotte. She has shared so much of herself with me, and I have avoided sharing as much as possible. Not to be cruel. But to remain in control. Control of my heart. And control of the future.

But how long can I put this off? Wouldn't it be best if I just ripped the bandage from the wound and exposed everything? Yes, that is what the logical part of me says. The proverbial angel on my shoulders tells me it's best to get it over with.

I take a deep breath and prepare for the conversation we should have had a while ago. "Mags…"

When she doesn't respond, I gaze down at her. My silent prayer answered when I hear her rhythmic breathing. Inhaling deep, I calm my nervous heart.

As ready as I believe I am, the relief coursing through me is a sign I wasn't as ready to share as I thought. I am ready for our worlds to become one, but I can't help thinking it may be too soon for her. All I know is that my heart and soul need her. And I can't imagine a day without her.

So I hold off once again. Tuck away my past a little longer. And I vow to tell her at some point, just not now.

The credits of the movie scroll on the screen before I shut the television off. Twisting, I scoop her into my arms and carry her to bed. She looks so angelic and fragile as her head graces the pillow. I am lost. Lost in this woman.

She stirs a bit as I slip under the covers, rolling onto her side to face me. A sweet hum vibrates from her body when she comes into contact with me. As if that's what she needs before falling asleep.

"I love you." The words I meant to say in my head suddenly roll off my tongue.

Her eyes pop open, looking at me as if she doesn't know me. Her forehead scrunches, and her eyes pull tight. I have no idea what she is thinking. That thought alone has my pulse soaring and my skin prickling.

There has only been one other woman I have ever said those words to. Only one other woman who made me feel as if

I had a purpose in this life. Only one other woman who captivated every part of me.

But that woman... she no longer exists. Only my memory of her.

I also can't compare my love for Charlotte versus my love for Mags. The two are incomparable. I don't want to tarnish Charlotte or the wonderful memories I have of her. At one point in my life, Charlotte was my everything. But the way my heart sings for Mags... She is the sun. And I have only known the moon before I knew her.

Mags' eyes dart back and forth between mine for several rapid heartbeats and three heavy breaths. She places a hand on my cheek, as I watch her lids draw back together and drift off once more, saying nothing beforehand.

How could she just fall back asleep after hearing my declaration? Not that I expect for her to come right out and respond in kind. But some sort of response would be good—positive or not.

I stare down at her sleeping form, my gut mangling into odd shapes. Pain seeping into my bones. And for the first time in years, fear swallows me whole.

CHAPTER 21

MAGDALENA

The weekend flew by in a whirlwind. You could feel the change of the seasons happening, and we took advantage of the beautiful, crisp weather by doing just about everything we could outdoors. Autumn brought with it a sense of vigor and joy. It's the time of year with my favorite holidays and get-togethers.

Throughout the weekend, though, I was on edge. Those three words. Did he really say *those* three words to me? I'm still not sure if I had been awake or dreaming. No matter how much I try to resurrect the moment, it's still foggy in my mind's eye, and I can't be certain it was real. The only thing absolute... I didn't say anything afterward.

Not. One. Single. Word.

Does that make me a horrible person? Guilt has rested on my shoulders like a pair of red horns all weekend and over the last few days. I'm lost in the cycle of *what should I do?* And it is on religious repeat.

Dream or reality, I should have at least opened my mouth and responded. Like every other reasonable person. Why do I have some odd inability to not express myself? It's simple routine for the other seven-plus billion people on the planet. So why not me?

And in this exact moment, I pledge I will say something to him this evening at dinner. It's not as if I don't have strong feelings for him. I just have trouble spewing out the infamous *l* word. Telling someone I love them is not something I just hand out. Sure, I vocalize my love to Lessa and Lena all the time. But it's different. I have known them since grade school.

The only other people I've told I loved them are gone. Not as if my parents chose to leave me. I loved them fiercely and it wasn't enough to keep them alive. Instinct says what I feel for Geoff is love, but the guardian of my heart screams that love only hurts us. She holds me hostage, whispering words like *loss* and *pain*. That same guardian reminds me that Geoff still holds back from telling me more about his past. Not just about Charlotte, but also with any other part of his life. How can he expect me to reciprocate such devotion if he won't let me in?

Is he intentionally avoiding the subject? Is he intentionally not sharing, but has an expectation I do? It all just feels so lopsided.

A raw fury simmers inside me. It's a mix of frustration and anger and dejection. And it strikes me like a bolt of lightning to my heart.

If I told Geoff I love him, would I lose him too?

And a whole new level of panic rises in my chest, squeezing my heart like a rag doll. Constricting my airways and crippling me. Ignoring his declaration can't continue. But I'm at a loss on what to say.

What if I was dreaming and I ruin us?

WELCOME
to
LAKE LAVENDER

With a few hours remaining on my shift at Statice, the center receives a call. A teenage girl will be brought in within the hour. The doctors don't reveal much of her backstory in our briefing but indicate she and I would pair well together. Before the group separates, a manila folder is set on the table in front of me. My fingers run over the file, reluctant to peel it open. But this isn't about me, so I open it up and reveal the inner contents.

I freeze. I'm a slab of carved marble. An unyielding statue. That is until warm wetness slides down my cheek. I can't breathe. Or speak. And somehow, I can't control the rivers flowing down either side of my face.

Nicole, the girl assigned to me, was involved in a car accident. Both her parents passed at the scene as she was rushed to the emergency room, unconscious. When she was taken to the hospital, she had no idea she was riding alone.

This hits close to home. Too close. *Can I do this?*

Yes, I can do this. I need to do this. This is one of the main reasons I chose this profession. To help others in the same way I was years ago. The same way I am today.

"*Mags.* Are you okay?" A warm embrace startles me.

I glance up at a pair of hazel eyes loaded with concern. Beatrice. My surrogate mother.

"I just need a moment. I wish they wouldn't spring things like this on us. Less than an hour before the kid comes in, too. How am I supposed to be mentally prepared?"

Her hug a tremendous comfort, she embraces me a moment longer. "You've had a lot on your plate recently. It's okay if you don't take on this girl's case. We have more counselors now. I can pass her on to one of them."

As we break away, her hands take mine. She watches me, concern flitting her eyes. "I've got this. But for once, would it kill them to give us more time? It would make things easier for everyone," I ramble.

"I'm right there with ya. I've nagged them more than a dozen times, but we see how that's working," she teases.

I laugh. "Yeah, but I'm sure if you keep at it, they'll cave. I would." Because Beatrice is a force to be reckoned with. She is fire and challenge and obstinance.

We sit quietly a moment, and I can feel Beatrice's eyes on me. Her concern for me evident, but I don't want to let anyone down. Not Beatrice. And not the kids here.

"Well, you take all the time you need, sweetheart. If you need more when she arrives, just say the word, and I'll find a way to delay the introduction."

I am so thankful for Beatrice. Not only was she once my mentor through this process, but we developed an irreplaceable bond over the years. My life would not be what it is today without her guidance, support, and loving words. I owe her a lifetime of love and gratitude.

"Thank you, Beatrice. I'm going to sit here a bit and read over her file. Will you please let me know when she's here?"

She pats my shoulder. "Certainly, sweetheart. And if you're not ready, you better tell me so." Her forehead bunches in a way that reminds me of a stern mother.

"I will, I promise."

I have thumbed through the file a few times, shutting the folder after each time. The first was, more or less, a brief scan of pictures. The second, I read the short bio—I always end up adding a novel to those bios. The third was to read her story.

Every folder always contains a brief of how the youth came into our care. Short and sweet. But I'll scour for more details. I have to be able to talk with this girl. To understand where her head is at. To know the correct way to respond to however she is handling life.

My lungs expand as I recall my first day at the center and remember the first talk Beatrice and I shared.

"Hello, Magdalena, my name is Beatrice. I wish we could be meeting under better circumstances. But it's still nice to meet you," the woman soothes, her large frame obstructing my view of everything.

I peek up at the lady standing in front of me and a warmth radiates from the sincere smile as her cheeks plump.

My eyes drop back to my hands that bounce with the constant movement of my legs and feet. I don't understand what is happening. Why am I here? All I know is I want to go home.

"Hi. When can I go home?" I ask the gentle woman named Beatrice.

"May I?" Her hand gestures to the spot next to me. I grant her permission to sit beside me. "Magdalena..."

"Mags. You can call me Mags."

"Thank you, Mags. Sweetheart, it might be a little while before you're allowed to go back home. That's not my decision. That's up to the doctor. They need to make sure you will be taken care of if you go home. Your father is very upset right now. You understand, don't you?"

I nod. A damp, hotness pours down my cheeks, and it's not long before a few tears break the dam. I am so tired of crying. I just want this nightmare to be over already.

I run the back of my long-sleeved forearm over my cheeks, drying up the tears as I study her face. She is so gentle in appearance—her eyes tender but not laden with pity. Her presence is soothing and I am more at ease in this moment, the tears slowing. "Okay. I don't know if you talk to them. But if you do, please tell them I have people I can stay with, or that can stay with me. Other than my dad."

"I will, sweetheart. I'm happy to hear you have other special people in your life. They will also be important to have around now. Keep them close." Her words resonate with me, and I know they will for years to come. Keep them close.

Out of nowhere, I have an urge to hug her, so I do. I wrap my arms around her and squeeze as if I'll never hug another soul in my life. Her arms embrace me in a manner reminding me of my mother, the warmth soothing away some of the hurt. "I will, I promise."

Depending on what is happening in my life, that memory sometimes seems not so long ago, and other times is many lifetimes away.

Lessa and Lena—and their families—have always been my primary support system. Although some years were tougher than others, we always kept in contact. After Mom died, Dad was a mess. So, I stayed with Lessa and Lena when he was having a bad day. And when Dad had his stroke, they would come over every week and hang with me. Because I refused to leave his side.

But no one helped me like Beatrice. No one's love compared to hers. On my worst days, she hugged and never spoke a word. On my best days, she hugged me and asked all the questions my mom would have. She is the reason why I decided to take psychology in college.

I owe her the world.

And then some.

And although she encouraged me like any mother would, I let her down. I promised I would keep everyone close. But when it came right down to it, I failed.

When I think back to all the time I spent with Lessa, Lena, or Beatrice, one common denominator stands out. They all initiated our time together. Lessa and Lena came over to my house regularly after my dad had his stroke and I refused to leave his side. Beatrice occasionally called or stopped by when she hadn't heard from me in weeks. Because amidst all the craziness, I never checked in with anyone.

Why did I shut everyone out? I also did it to Dad after Mom died, now that I really think about it. There were so many days when I curled up in a ball on my bed and never left my room. Days when I should have been talking to Dad, because he missed Mom more than I did. He needed me more than I did him, and I shut him out. How selfish of me.

The folder in my hands heavy, but a weight I can bear. Can I do this? Can I be the base of comfort and support for this young woman? Am I capable of being this girl's Beatrice? Am I capable of being there for her while she copes with losing her parents?

I want to say yes. I want to be strong enough to be the person she needs. To show her life will continue after this. But how can I show her if I ignored life for so many years myself?

Scanning the pages once more, I remind myself... *I can do this.* I repeat it over and over until it sinks in and I believe nothing else. Because I *can* do this. Not just for her, but for me as well.

Nicole and I sit on a bench in the center's outdoor garden. It is a quiet place adorned with trees and flowers that provides privacy without being alone. And is the best thinking space on the grounds. The only thing that has changed over the years is how tall the trees are.

Our conversation has been a slow-going—I do most of the talking, as most of the counselors usually do in the beginning. Our connection, even if she is unaware of it, helps make our first meeting flow smoother than some others.

"So, what happens now?" Nicole asks.

During our talk, I learned Nicole has family in Florida. An aunt, uncle, and two cousins close to her in age. She hasn't seen them in five years, but they talked on a regular basis—her mom and aunt were sisters.

"Now I let the doctors know about your aunt and uncle. We'll call them and figure out how to move forward." Although, I'm sure someone already knew about her living family and has made calls.

Nicole slumps in her seat, tears rolling down her cheeks. "I'm so sick of crying," she sniffles.

God, I remember feeling this exact way. Remember thinking I'd dehydrate from all the tears I shed. Tears were cathartic but exhausting.

"I know you are, sweetie. Eventually, you'll cry less. It may not be for a while, but I promise you will. You'll never forget your mom and dad, but you'll learn how to live without them. And move forward. By creating new bonds and friendships. Strong ones that'll mean more."

Her bloodshot eyes question mine. "How can you know?"
Just be yourself.

"Because it happened for me." Although, I refuse to admit how many years I cried. Refuse to share how I shut myself away from the world. I am thankful Lessa and Lena stayed close, even if the frequency shrunk each year and they initiated most of our time together.

Epiphany strikes and I slap myself mentally. *Who am I to give this girl advice when I haven't always followed my own?* It took me years to follow the advice I just gave her. Too many years. Yes, I was close with Lena, Lessa, and Beatrice. Lucky for me, they continued to force their way into my life. If they hadn't, I would be alone. Because I never made an attempt to bring anyone else into my life. Not once. The constant fear of growing close to someone else always hindered me.

Nicole cannot follow my path. She can't stop living. Not like I did. For far too many years, I allowed my pain to rule my life and decisions. However possible, I needed to guide Nicole away from doing the same. I needed to guide her to a place where smiles and laughter and joy were abundant.

I glance at my watch. We have been in the garden for a little over two hours. As vital as downtime is for me, I wouldn't dare leave Nicole earlier. Her need for comfort, love, and solace is in my hands. There is no way I can walk away from her for selfish reasons. As of today, I am one of her new lifelines.

I give her time to process everything we discussed how the program at Statice works. How each young woman or man is paired with a counselor. How many visits they had with their counselor each week. Usually, in the beginning, the sessions would be a minimum of three times each week. If there is ever a day when the youth isn't scheduled to have time with their counselor, but needed time, arrangements would be made.

Every person's life and story different, and the center is a firm believer in giving each person what they require for recovery. This is a stressful time and Statice recognizes this, hands down.

"Let's head inside," I suggest.

Nicole nods and we leave our spot in the garden. Her sad eyes look everywhere but at me. She isn't ready to share everything with me yet, and that's okay. But one day in the future, she will share everything with me. Tears and sorrow, pain and, one day, laughter. I will become a stronghold in her world. Someone she can rely on when no one else is available. Listen to every word she speaks, whether it's sad or happy. Patience is one of the most significant and challenging parts of this job. But I promise to give her as much patience as is necessary.

We walk back inside and go our separate ways—she walks to the room the center has set up for her, and I make my preparations to leave. She won't remain at the center for long since she has family. I'm sure the center has begun the process of having her transferred into their custody—something Statice always aims for if at all feasible. But staying here and not being surrounded by familiarity is one of the hardest parts. Her home would swamp her with memories of her parents, but is more desirable than a foreign, doctor-like facility.

As I walk toward the exit, Beatrice stops me. "How's Nicole doing?"

"Sad. Confused. Wants to go home," I share.

"It breaks my heart to see these kids like this."

"Me too, but it doesn't last forever. We move past it."

Beatrice gives me a knowing look. She won't say it, but she's subliminally telling me to take my own advice. Because it wasn't until a couple months back that I did this, after years of sitting at home. "Yes, we do."

I ask if the center knew about her family in Florida. Beatrice shares that is one of the reasons she stopped me before leaving. Her family has been contacted and arrangements have been made for Nicole to move in with them. The catch? I will be chauffeuring her and helping her acclimate to her new life.

"If it's too stressful, someone else can take her. I worry about you and the workload you've taken on," Beatrice confesses.

I shake my head. "I can do this. Besides, we've already formed a bond. I'd rather not make her any more uncomfortable."

Beatrice studies me with her concerned mother eyes, looking for signs this case is eating at me. When she seems satisfied, she replies. "Then it's settled. You and Nicole are headed to Florida, day after tomorrow. I'll email you the details."

"Thanks, Beatrice." I take a few tentative steps closer to her and wrap my arms around her mid-section. It has been far too long since we've hugged, more my doing than hers. "I've never told you how much you mean to me. I've never really thanked you for always being there for me."

"Oh, sweetheart. You don't need to thank me. I do all of this because I love you. And all the other kids that walk through those doors."

Even now, when I'm trying to step up and be brave, Beatrice consoles me. It makes me love her that much more. "But I do need to thank you. For always being there when I needed someone to talk with. For checking in on me, because even though I said I would keep everyone close, I didn't. I unintentionally secluded myself from everyone who mattered. And I still am."

Beatrice holds me at arm's length and stares at me, her eyes softening by the corners as her lips curve up. "Yes, you are. But at least now you have figured it out. Some never do. It may have taken you longer than you like, but at least it happened. I'm proud of you, sweetheart."

A new sense of relief rushes throughout my body, and for the first time in several years, I choose to be someone different. Someone other than the girl whose parents died and everyone pitied her. Instead, I choose to help Nicole become what I couldn't—a girl who learns to live again.

Before leaving, I hug Beatrice one last time. "Thank you," I whisper. "I'll see you soon."

When we break apart, I walk slower to the exit, my mind all over the map. Beatrice watches me leave, her observation making me edgy and nervous. But with my new realization, I also have a renewed sense of confidence. There is only one thing I don't know the answer to. One last thing that makes me nervous.

How do I explain to Geoff why I'm flying to Florida? Better yet, how will he take it?

It seems as if my drive to Geoff's never happened, but here I am, standing at his door, hand prepared to knock. I stand here, hesitant, and longing for time alone to process my time with Nicole today. Even though I was only with her a couple of hours, a series of memories and revelations awoke in me, and I haven't had time to process them before jumping back into the present.

A voice in the back of my head continues to nag me since I met Geoff. A voice barking at me to tell him more about my past. Right now, that voice is screaming. The only reason I've held back from sharing more with people, including Geoff, is because I don't want to be pitied.

No one wants to be the person always thought of as *the girl who lost her parents so young* or *the girl who stopped living to take care of her dying father*. No one wants to be hugged extra tight by someone who has no clue what it feels like to lose someone who means the world to you. No one wants to be reminded repeatedly of that time.

I extend my hand forward, ready to knock when the door opens. Geoff stands before me, his forehead worrying into deep lines, his head cocked in question. Questions I need to dig up the strength to answer.

"Sorry. I was about to knock. Just had a funky day and was trying to clear my thoughts before I came in."

Relaxation returns his features to that handsome face I love to look at. "It's fine. I was just wondering if you were okay. I'd heard your car door a few minutes ago, but then nothing else. You sure you're okay?"

"I'll be okay. Today was just an unexpected day. I'll tell you more in a bit." Clarity strikes me like lightning, and I register it's time I share this part of myself with Geoff. The part I keep locked tight.

We share strong feelings for one another, and if I keep this hidden, we will never be able to move forward. We may not want to be defined by our history, but it's who we are. And I now know it's imperative I share, grow, and move on with others who embrace me.

His smile warms my chest before his arms wrap around me, encompassing me and taking away every worry resting in my bones. It is difficult to translate the sense of serenity I have when Geoff holds me. He is my serotonin, coursing through my veins and making my world better.

We meander inside, fingers woven together. He continues cooking while I sit on a stool and watch his every move. His every movement in the kitchen is effortless, and I wish for a fraction of that ease.

Dinner passes without much conversation, more from my doing. A million thoughts run laps in my head, trying to sort out the best way to talk with him about my parents. I have told him a little about Mom, but nothing about Dad. Something else comes to mind, too. How do I handle telling him about my upcoming trip with Nicole? I'll be away for two weeks, give or take. If the knot twisting in my gut is any indication, the news isn't going to go over smoothly.

Geoff joins me on the couch after putting the last of the dishes in the dishwasher. Worry emanates from his aura in waves. My silence surely isn't helping the matter.

I have to dispel his concern, although what I plan to say won't help. *Deep breath in, deep breath out.* "I'm sorry I've been so quiet tonight. I promise it isn't anything about us."

Absorbing this, he gazes at me and takes a moment before responding. "Is there anything I can do to help? I'm here for you, no matter what. You know that, right?"

The warmth of his words plucks at my heartstrings and encompasses me like a soft blanket on a cold day. I allow myself a moment of this. Him, us, together, completely wrapped up in each other. Giving each other what we yearn. Somewhere along the line, it's begun to feel like he is the only thing I need.

Whether it was a dream or not, he loves me. And his love gives me strength and courage, the two things I need most for what I was about to say. What I am about to do. Because I am about to become the most vulnerable I have ever been.

"I got a new case at the center today. A teenage girl whose story closely resembles my own." The squeeze of his arms, pulling me impossibly closer to him, is a balm. "The center paired her with me because of that fact. At first, I was a mess. My tears wouldn't stop. After talking with Beatrice, my former counselor and now supervisor, I assured her I would be okay but needed time before meeting her. I calmed myself down, switched to counselor mode and went out to meet her."

His thumb brushes my cheek, wiping the moisture I didn't realize had fallen. He doesn't say a word. He just holds me, listening, waiting for me to continue. Knowing I will when I am ready.

I inhale and push forward. "Talking with her today stirred up so many memories of my past. Memories that have held me prisoner for years. Memories that have kept me from moving on, from growing, from loving. And it hit me. How I don't want my past to dictate my future. And how I move forward. It's time I try."

He stares at me as if he is trying to read my thoughts. If it were that simple, I would spill everything to him. But that would be the easy way out. And the easy way isn't always the best way. The hard way is difficult for a reason. Getting things out is an opportunity to let happiness flood back in. At least that is what I'm hoping. Out with the bad, in with the good.

His fingers graze my chin as he brings his mouth to mine, leaving a simple, sweet kiss in its wake. "Whatever you want to share, I leave that completely in your hands."

I stare at him, long and hard, for a minute. This man astounds me left and right, day in and day out. "I can never thank you enough for that. It means more than I can ever say. You have been the biggest change in my life in years. At times, I wish we could've met sooner. But I know everything happens when it's meant to."

"You never need to thank me. You being here with me, that is all the thanks I need."

Unsure how to respond, I opt to leave it. Instead, I elect to share the part of my life I'm sure he has curiosities over.

I gaze down at my fumbling fingers in my lap. "I'm not sure where to begin..." My childhood full of so many happy memories, overridden with the darkest. My parents were amazing and devoted. Maria and Jacob Bishop. Loyal to each other and dedicated to me. I couldn't imagine better parents.

"My mom had the most compassionate heart and would help a stranger. My dad, although his job tested his sanity, was the gentlest man I knew. We went everywhere together. Both my parents were involved in school functions and fundraisers, always wanting to give back to others."

Geoff plants his hand on my knee and squeezes. "They sound wonderful."

I nod. "In elementary school, I met Alessandra and Helena —Lessa and Lena. We were instant friends and managed to make all our parents' friends, too. As a trio of families, we did so much together, like one huge family.

"When I was seven-years-old, I told my mom I wanted to become a ballerina after watching The Nutcracker for the first time." Geoff freezes beside me, and I make a mental note to ask him why. "I think we both thought I would change my mind after a few classes, but I kept going and she encouraged me every step of the way. There was a time when I thought ballet would be my career."

That dream faded when I lost my mom.

"Just before Thanksgiving, my high school boyfriend broke up with me. Needless to say, I was devastated. Things had been great in my eyes. He thought otherwise." Looking back now, I guess my thoughts were clouded by the idea of love. "I'd given him my virginity, and I thought that meant more to him than it apparently did."

"Jerk," Geoff mumbles beside me, shifting in his seat. His comment makes me smile.

When the breakup happened, my mom was the one person who helped me get through it all. I told her everything, and she never passed judgment. All she did was give me love. I think that's what her purpose on this Earth was.

I still remember *the* night like it was yesterday. "A couple weeks later, my dad and I were at home. Dad was cooking, and I was doing homework, waiting for Mom to get home from work. Dad finished making dinner and asked if I would set the table. When I grabbed the plates, I remember looking at the clock—six-forty-seven-pm—and noting it was late and how I was surprised Mom wasn't home yet. The latest she'd ever gotten home was between six o'clock and quarter after."

Geoff clutches my knee as if he knows what I'll say next. I rest my hand over his, loving how supportive he is.

"Dad was bringing the food to the table when the phone rang. He answered it, and I watched his face turn a ghostly shade of white. I'd never been so afraid in my life. He mumbled a few words into the handset and then disconnected the call. The ashen look had not dissipated. All he said was 'Get your jacket, we need to go to the hospital.'"

I've never really known if he knew my mom's status at that moment, he never told me. My dad drove frantically to the hospital. It all happened so fast, I don't remember the drive at all. Just that my dad was distraught.

I pause, tears rolling down my cheeks. Geoff swipes them away with his thumbs, pressing kisses in their place. When he leans back, I share the next chapter of my past.

"Dad and I were not the same after that night. We ignored Christmas twelve days later. I cried for weeks. We relied on each other and kept in constant contact, sharing where we were at all times and when we'd be coming or going.

"After what seemed like a thousand daily therapy sessions for us both, we were finally less teary-eyed. We knew it would never be the same. How could it? But we were on the path to better days."

We celebrated my birthday as if it was the most monumental day of the year. For Halloween, Dad thought it would be fun to have my friends over and do some scary movie marathon. He was right, it was great. As Thanksgiving crept up on us, we were invited over to Lessa's house. Between the three families that became one over the previous decade, we had a massive feast. One that will never be forgotten.

Life was less meek, but I still missed Mom. My birthdays and graduation were the most difficult. "Shortly after second semester of my sophomore year in college, I headed home after a study session. Dad was stopping at the store but would be home soon after me. Winter had been pounding the roads with snow that season. On his way home, my dad suffered a massive stroke and hit a tree.

"It was my turn to take a call from the police. I was a basket case. All I kept thinking was *I can't lose him too.* When I got to the hospital, everything blurred. The time I waited for his diagnosis dragged on for hours. When I finally spoke with the doctor and learned of his stroke, I was sad to learn he'd be bedridden the rest of his life. But I was also happy I still had him."

Geoff draws circles over my palm with his thumb. "I'm glad you had him too." Something in Geoff's expression piques my interest. No sadness. No emotion whatsoever. Just... neutrality. And I don't know why, but it twists a knot in my gut.

"Over the next two-and-a-half years, life as I knew it changed. I still attended college, only from home. The only time I left the house was if a nurse came by to relieve me. Which was once a week, and I used that time to grocery shop. Lessa and Lena would stop by and check on me. We had dinners at my house once or twice a month, but they had busy lives."

One day, I checked on my dad as per usual. He hadn't been eating much and I was growing more and more worried. When I walked into the room, he looked happy. He was smiling. Not the smile I remembered, but a new version of it. 'Hi Daddy. Are you feeling better today?' I'd said to him. I wove my fingers with his and smiled back at him. Seeing him happy brought tears to my eyes.

At that moment, less than an hour before he died, my dad soothed me and wiped away my tears with his good hand. He told me to go out and live my life.

"It didn't hit me right away, but on the day he died, he was saying goodbye to me. He told me how proud he was of me and all I had done. When he said he loved me for the tenth time, I knew something wasn't right."

Dad asked me if I remembered the family attorney's name. I reluctantly answered him. Because why would he ask me that? Why would he bring that up out of left field?

"And then he said something I will never forget. 'Mags, I see your mother. Everything's going to be okay. We love you so much.' I kept saying to him that he was going to make it. He had to because I didn't think I could live without him. Minutes later, he closed his eyes and never opened them again."

Geoff sat silently beside me. No tears, unlike me. His expression still as neutral as before, but he watched me close. Locked on my every tear, sob, and tremble.

Silence hovers around us. I just dumped a lot in his lap all at once. I'm sure he'll need time to wrap his head around it all. I would, if I were in his position.

A moment later, Geoff clutches both my hands in his. "Thank you for telling me. I knew a little of how your mom and dad passed, but hearing it from you means so much."

I jerk away from him, my face scrunching. "What do you mean you knew? I only mentioned my mom's death to you once. Not how. And not my dad at all." My stomach churns and I wrap my arms around my mid-section.

Guilt muddles his face. Under my scrutiny, he opens and closes his mouth a couple of times. The third time he opens his mouth, he says, "I, uh…" Then he's locked down tight again.

"You what?" My heart is pounding. Why does this feel like an attack?

"I, uh, Googled you. After reading the article in the paper," he mumbles.

Did I hear him correctly? God, I hope not. "Why didn't you tell me you read the article?"

Geoff scratches his head, looking everywhere but at me. "I didn't know what to say."

I wait for him to look at me as I try to calm down. "Maybe something like *hey, Mags, I read that article in the paper you did an interview for. Want to talk about it?*" I pause a moment, my blood like lava. "That would have been the adult thing to do."

"Look, I'm sorry. Please forgive me. I just… I wanted to know more about you."

I stand and step away from the couch, my eyes blazing through him. Is he serious? I'm seething. "So, instead of asking me like a mature adult, you *Googled* me? Why would you do that?" I think I'm going to be sick.

The relief I'd discovered moments ago sharing my past, it

was long gone. Why wouldn't he just talk to me? Ask me whatever questions he had?

Geoff stands and steps closer to me. I take another step back. He hangs his head, a loud huff escaping him. "I'm sorry. I just…"

"What? Wanted to invade my privacy? Because that's what you did. You invaded it. Big time!" Who the hell does he think he is?!

"Sorry. It's just…" He pauses, and this time I don't interrupt him. "You were so closed off, so hesitant. I didn't know what land mines were where, and you wouldn't let me in. But you're so important to me—how could I keep from blowing things up without knowing where to step? I couldn't let you leave me, not after Charlotte left me."

I shake my head at him. He cannot be serious. "Geoff, losing Charlotte was difficult for you. I get that. But doing what you did to me. That's not going to bring us closer together. A violation like that, it divides us. It breaks the trust I have in you. You could've asked me, rather than *Googling* me."

"But would you have told me? I don't think so. I waited for you to tell me on your own, I gave you all the space you wanted, but after a while, it felt like that would never happen!"

I am so angry with him right now. I can't even think straight. With everything happening with Nicole, I didn't need this additional stress. This is utter bullshit.

"Oh, because you're such an open book? What do I actually know about you? You have this lopsided standard that I need to share everything and you get to remain tight-lipped. I know next to nothing about you—from basic stuff like your favorite color to major things like where you're from. I'm no relationship guru, but I know enough to say that's not how it works.

I... I can't do this right now." I shake my head. "Maybe we need to take a break. I have to fly to Florida the day after tomorrow with my new case and get her settled. I'll probably be there a couple weeks. That gives us both time apart to figure out where to go from here. But I'll be honest, this doesn't sit well with me."

In an instant, Geoff stands a breath from me. Worry slashes his face like a scar. Fear floods his eyes. "Mags, no. I'm sorry. It was wrong and I shouldn't have done it. I'll never do anything like this again."

"Regardless, I still have to go to Florida," I say, walking toward the door. "Take the time and think over things."

When I reach for the doorknob, Geoff's desire for control appears as he steps between me and the door, blocking me. "Please, Mags. Don't go. Stay so we can talk about this. I can't lose you."

I don't want to hurt him. But what he did is unforgivable. Traveling with Nicole is what we both need. Time apart. Time to see how we genuinely feel. Time to see what life is like without each other.

"I'm sorry. But I have to go. Please move."

He stares at me and I glare at him in return. Seconds later, he hangs his head as his frame slumps and he steps aside. His guilt radiates off him like a wayward storm. But this is the right thing to do. Especially if we want a chance at a future.

And without a backward glance, I walk out the door.

CHAPTER 22

GEOFFREY

God, I miss Mags.

It has been three days since she poured her heart out to me, and I admitted to basically stalking her. Three days since she walked out my door without looking back. Three days since her hand caressed mine.

I haven't been able to catch my breath since she left.

I don't know which way is up, but I sure as hell know which way is down because I'm plummeting into it head-on. It's as if I've been drowning. Sinking deeper and deeper with each passing day.

I remain glued to my phone as if I expect Mags to jump out of it. My hands grip the device like a lifeline, my silent pleas begging her to come back. Praying she'll leap out of the phone —even if only in words. Come sit beside me again, wrapped in my arms, where she belongs. Give me her strength, so I can make this better.

Sleep evades me—I'm lucky if I get an hour or two a night. And focusing at work is an absolute joke.

When Logan checked in with me yesterday, his hackles

were on high alert at my somber mood. I blew him off, telling him I was just in a bad mood. He wasn't buying it.

Logan, Owen, and I had been friends since college. Owning a business together also meant we knew each other well. Too well. At times, it worked to our advantage.

Now is not one of those times.

After thirty minutes of monotonous conversation yesterday afternoon, I caved. I spilled everything that happened between me and Mags. The good, and the ugly. How things had been wonderful. And how I ruined it with my insatiable curiosity and need for control.

They knew about Charlotte and the dark depression I sunk into after losing her. They also knew that's why I never stayed with one woman. Because if I lost someone else, I'd go off the deep end.

Had I lost Mags? Maybe. Maybe not. *God, I hope not.*

She said we needed a break. Time apart to think. With her out of town, there was no choice but to have time apart. I want to fix things with her, only I wasn't sure how.

Right now, Logan and Owen sit in my living room. Hooting and hollering at the football game on television. After my woe-is-me babble, Logan thought it a good idea for the three of us to hang out like old times. This was their version of helping. Or so I guessed. And as much as I want to be a good host, I don't have it in me to entertain anyone. Hell, how can I make others happy when I'm incapable of doing so myself?

"Bro, you need another beer?" Logan asks, his eyes zeroed in on the screen.

"Nah, I'm good," I mutter, peeling the label from my brown bottle. I still have more than half my beer left.

Owen stops watching the game and peeks over his shoulder at me, his eyes etched with worry. His features expressing all the words he resists saying. I am thankful for his reservation, even if talking was what I should be doing.

The room goes silent and I glance up at the television, discovering Logan muted it. His elbows rest on his knees as he hangs his head and shakes it. And I sense what's about to happen.

"This has to end," Logan states, eyes locked on mine.

"What?" I toss out, playing coy. It's no secret what he's referring to, but I refuse to say it aloud.

"This." Logan points at me, his finger indicating up and down my body. "You look like shit. I understand you're in a bad place with Mags, but you're not even trying. Owen and I have offered to listen and give you whatever advice we can. But how can we do that if you don't let us in?"

I shift my focus from Logan to Owen, and he nods. Without uttering a word, Owen says so much. I read his worry in the lines on his forehead. His sadness for me in his eyes. "We just want to know you're okay," Owen states, solemn.

"I'm *fine*," I snap at them both. What a stupid fucking word. *Fine*. I want to write that word on a piece of paper, then rip it into a million little bits.

Logan pops up from the leather recliner, stepping closer to me. "Really?" he barks out. "Because you look far from *fine*. I love you, man. We both do. And we want nothing more than for you to be happy. But how the hell can we help you get there when you shut us out?"

I gawk at the pair of them. They've never been so impassioned before unless it involved work. They're coming at me full force, guns blazing. These are my best friends; they're only doing this because they love me. I should cut them some slack and listen to what they have to say. Maybe heed their advice.

"She's not Charlotte," Owen whispers, and I flinch. The

truth cutting me open. "You may not be in the best place, but she's still here. You have a chance to make things right." He's right, and all know it.

Water pools in my eyes, my throat tight at the comparison of the only two women I've loved. "How?" I croak. "How can I make this better? I screwed up. Huge. That doesn't just fade away. She's not going to just forget about it."

I lean forward and rest my forearms on my legs, hanging my head. Sliding my fingers through my messy strands, I press my palms against my eyes.

How could I possibly fix this? It's like losing Charlotte all over again. But this time, I initiated the stab wound to my heart. This is the worst pain I have ever experienced. And I am less in control than before.

Logan sits down beside me. "Look, man," he says, and I tip my face in his direction. "She is *not* Charlotte. Mags said she wanted time for both of you to think and see where things go. Give her the time, but check in at the end of the week. Keep it short and sweet. Tell her you miss her. Ask how she's doing in Florida. Maybe she'll respond. Maybe she won't. Either way, at least she knows she's on your mind."

I groan, "I am so bad at this. How do I get her to trust me again? If I promise to never do it again, why would she believe me?" I run my fingers through my hair, clenching them into fists and yanking the strands.

"It's not going to happen overnight, but you have to keep trying. You said you told her about Charlotte," Owen says, and I nod. "But how *much* have you told her?"

In my opinion, I shared the vital parts of me and Charlotte with Mags. But maybe I didn't. Mags opened her heart and exposed every raw feeling she had. She shared major chunks of herself. Me? I gave her the outlined version of my time with Charlotte.

"Not much," I answer. "I told her how long we were together and what happened to her. That's it."

Owen pats my back, not removing his hand for a beat. "You need to tell her more. As difficult as it is, you need to show her that part of your life. How things were before Charlotte died. And how things were after. It's going to hurt. But how can you move forward if you don't?"

He is right. They both are. If I want any semblance of a future with Mags, I need to be more vulnerable than before. It is going to be hard as hell, but to save what Mags and I have, I need to rip my scars wide open. Rehash wounds that I buried long ago.

A moment of silence wraps around us before Logan unmutes the television. His way of saying the conversation is finished. While Logan and Owen continue watching the game, I zone out. Trying to come up with what to say to Mags.

She deserves to know about Charlotte and why losing her made me how I am today. Maybe that is a step in the direction of earning her trust back. I earn Mags' trust by being pure and raw and vulnerable.

But how do I talk about Charlotte without breaking into a million pieces. Over the last couple of weeks, she has been on my mind often. I love remembering her. But every time memories bubble up, sadness follows. The precise reason I block it all out. Traveling back down that hole again will do me no good. Maybe if I share Charlotte with Mags, the happy memories won't be overtaken by the tragic ones.

If I want a chance at any future with Mags, I must tear down my walls. If I truly love her, I need to bleed my truth to her. Tears and all.

A couple more days pass, and I grow more antsy. I have yet to message Mags but plan to do so after work today. Three hours ahead in Florida, I figure if I message between five and six she is more likely to see it.

And possibly answer.

I have zero expectations of her responding, but I'm hopeful.

God, I hope she answers.

Although work has kept me busy, my focus is shit. The papers on my desk look like foreign objects with caveman drawings and hieroglyphics scribbled on them. I have stared at the same piece of paper for the last ten minutes and it is all gibberish. Although I have done everything within my power, it's like I'm spiraling down the rabbit hole all over again. And that is not a good place to be.

Snap out of it, Lawson.

I shake my head before checking the time. Eleven-twenty-two. Another half hour, then lunch. And after lunch, I need to crank out this floorplan. It should consume the rest of my day. And if it doesn't, I will make it consume my day. Because distractions—not like the ones I had before Mags—are all I have right now.

And then… Then I will reach out to Mags.

CHAPTER 23

MAGDALENA

S weat rolls along the curve of my neck and down my chest. The first thought in my head—I am melting. Between the temperature and the humidity, I'm not sure which is worse. It was so beautiful outside, I decided to sit outside in the screened-in back porch. But obviously in Florida, the view from a window can be deceiving.

How do people live in this heat?

I packed pants and tops—short-sleeve, *thank God*—and thought I'd be good. But it turns out fall in Florida is warmer than our hottest summer day in Washington. If I wasn't so busy with Nicole, this would be pure misery.

My time with Nicole has been jam-packed. Not a single second has ticked by where we weren't getting her life in Florida situated.

Her aunt and uncle picked us up from the airport Friday morning and drove us to their home in St. Petersburg. After dropping off our belongings, we headed to the school Nicole would attend and registered her for classes. After a brief tour

I spent the weekend watching the family dynamic and making sure Nicole was comfortable in her new surroundings. So far, everything was good. Sadness lingered in Nicole's eyes, but she masked it with a smile. All I kept thinking was how brave she was. After dealing with so many changes all at once, her strength gave me hope. Hope that everything would be okay.

We talked for a few hours over the weekend, too. Taking walks in a park near her new home, we sat on a shady bench and I let her vent everything worrying her. Her parents being gone. What would happen to their home in Washington. Missing her friends. Attending a new school and making new friends.

I assured her, as best I could, that all would get sorted out. And nothing stopped her from talking with her friends back home. Although it may be some time before she sees them again.

My body is beyond tired, but the reward of helping her outweighs my exhaustion.

While she is attending her first day at St. Petersburg High School with one of her cousins, I located a counselor in the area to assume my role when I go home. After a brief conversation, I managed to get an appointment for Nicole and I with the new doctor later today.

"Would you like to go out and sight-see while Nicole is at school?" Nicole's aunt Marie asks as she steps out on to the porch and sets a glass of ice water in front of me.

"No, thank you."

Marie sits down in a chair opposite me and sips on her own water. She seems so at ease in this heat and it baffles me. I stare out into the family's back yard and try to get lost in the scenery like I do at home. Except it's so different. There are no mountains or sky-high trees in Florida. Instead, their yard is landscaped with a pond and fountain, multi-colored stones surrounding the border. Along the back wooden fence, several small palm trees and tropical plants sit in a bed of red mulch. Fresh cut grass and car pollution fill my nostrils and I have to wonder how anyone enjoys this.

But to each their own. It's not my place to judge who enjoys what and why.

"Well, if you change your mind, let me know. I don't get out of the house much, and it'd be nice to just walk around downtown with someone."

I nod, not wanting to appear rude.

The whole family has been wonderful. They refused to let me get a hotel, telling me they had plenty of room to accommodate. It's been nice to be in a house full of people again, and I can't help but think of how my life would have been different if my parents were still alive. Being here, seeing their family interaction—the hugs and I love you's and smiles—has me reminiscing over those I shared with my parents.

And Geoff. Although I have never told him I love him.

Do I love him? Part of me says yes, another says no.

It's not possible to ignore the magnetic pull we share. But his violation of my privacy was heinous, and not so easy to forgive. I want to forgive him. Want to believe he'll never do something like that again. But a voice inside me keeps repeating *how do you know.*

I don't. But giving up isn't the solution. It never has been.

"Want to talk about it?"

I stop staring at the palm trees sitting along the fence line and face her. "About what?"

"Whatever has you somewhere else. Sometimes it's nice to talk with someone not in the thick of it."

I study her a moment. *Could I talk with a stranger about me and Geoff?* It would be nice to confide in someone and get advice from a fresh perspective.

"I'm sorry I've been so distracted. Something came up before we left Washington. And I haven't had time to process it yet," I wince.

"No need to apologize. We all have stuff going on. But if you'd like to talk about it before you go, I'm here," she offers before rising and walking off.

It's nice she offered, and I may take her up on it, but I want to sort through my feelings on my own first.

Geoff and I haven't seen each other in almost a week. And I miss him like crazy, but at times I wonder if it is reciprocated. By now, I thought he would have tried calling or messaging. But there's been nothing. I keep telling myself he is just giving us the space I said we needed.

I hope that's it.

More than once, I have typed out a message to him. Deleting it a minute later. How can I express how I'm feeling if I haven't even dealt with it myself?

Maybe I will take Nicole's aunt up on her offer. Just not today. Perhaps tomorrow, when Nicole is at school again. After school today, we're meeting Nicole's new counselor. Her aunt and uncle will come with us and we'll have a group session to help Nicole with the transition.

In the blink of an eye, something strikes me. Here I am, helping a young woman share her story, her life, with others and I am falling short with that myself. Yes, I garnered the nerve to tell Geoff everything, but then I walked away. He may have done something wrong, but I sidestepped his every attempt at redemption. I opened myself up and shut him out within minutes.

How much longer would I need to spend with Nicole? Since arriving here, she was doing better. I remember being in a strange limbo. Tired of being pitied, of being hovered over, but also craving hugs and someone to tell me everything would be okay. I kept so much to myself, though. And I didn't want that to be Nicole.

I didn't want her life to mirror mine.

When we visit the counselor today, I will better gauge if I need to stay longer than another week. Secretly, I wish I could leave sooner. Nicole needs me, but now family surrounds her. And I have seen small changes since we arrived. When I leave, she will thrive. And that single thought lifts any remaining ounce of stress regarding how she will do when I leave.

The front door swings open, snapping me from my introspection. Nicole and her cousin walk through the door, laughing. A smile dons both their faces. My eyes well with joy, my heart swelling. *Nicole will be alright.* It's so wonderful to see her smile. To see her enjoying life.

After Geoff and I talk, I'm hoping we can share smiles again.

We head to the house after dinner—picking up Nicole's cousins after the session.

The first counseling session went well. Nicole appeared comfortable with the new counselor and having us all there. I will attend the next two sessions with her before leaving. All in all, her transition looks promising.

As we park in the driveway, my phone buzzes in my purse. Once I scoot from the third row of the SUV, I unlock my phone and see I have a message notification from Geoff.

Should I open it? Should I wait? I freeze in the driveway, staring at my phone screen, unsure.

Everyone except Marie walks into the house. She comes up beside me and pats my shoulder. It's a simple gesture, but welcome. "Why don't you walk to the back yard and sit on the swing. Give yourself some privacy," she says, gesturing to my phone.

I nod. "Thanks, Marie."

"I'm here, if you need me." It's all she says before walking inside the house.

I follow the dim path lights to the back yard, sitting on the hand-carved swing. I kick my feet a few times before opening the message, my stomach in knots. It's not just one message, it's two. Two large blocks of words filling the screen.

Deep breath in, deep breath out.

GEOFFREY

> Sorry if I'm interrupting you. Hope all is well and you're able to get things settled. I'm sending this message because it's the easiest way to tell you some things and not disrupt you. If you'll give me a chance, when you return, I'd like to better explain things.

GEOFFREY

> As simple as it would be to do it through a text, I would be a coward for doing so. Especially after your bravery. You don't need to answer me tonight. I wouldn't expect you to. But please give me an opportunity. That's all I ask.

I read the messages again and again. Hurt and regret hinting his words. Our time apart seizing my heart more each day. Tears pool in my eyes, my throat tightening. If anything, I just need an explanation for his actions.

Maybe after we talk, I will discover how to trust him again. At least I hope so. Because I want to.

CHAPTER 24
GEOFFREY

I bolt from the bed, drenched in sweat, and run to the bathroom. Bent at the waist, hands braced on my thighs, my stomach roils as I hover above the toilet.

Just when I think things can't get any worse, memories of Charlotte invade my dreams in the sickest way.

"Geoff, stop it!"

Charlotte smacks my hand away from the lilac-hued material. She is always a vision to behold before she goes on stage. Not a hair out of place, piled high and in the cute bun I love to tease her about. Her makeup darker than usual, but not unfavorable. Her pale pink points wrapped around her ankle and up her calf.

"You're going to be amazing out there tonight. Don't worry about the audience, just be yourself. I know you'll nail it."

I throw as much encouragement as possible her way. Tonight is a big deal. Judges from a few dance schools across the country are sitting in the audience. Tonight's performance is her audition. And she will have her choice of any of them.

"Where are you sitting?"

"I'll be in the second row, on your left."

She usually shut out the audience, but whenever she needs to feel grounded she looks for me. She once told me that I was her strength. I begged to differ. She is stronger than anyone I know. But I didn't argue with her.

"Okay. I'll find you before the curtain goes up."

I give her a small kiss on the cheek, not wanting to mess up her makeup. "I love you."

"Love you too. See you in a bit," she smiles and waves me away.

Before I exit backstage, I turn to catch one last glimpse of her. One leg propped on a barre, she is doing some last-minute stretches to warm her muscles. Her arms bow and flex as she shifts her weight. She's a princess. My princess. And the only thought I have at that moment is that one day I am going to marry her. And when she turns to look over her shoulder, it's no longer Charlotte. It's Mags.

That first dream had me dizzy. I woke to damp sheets and a racing heart. No matter how much I shook my head, I kept seeing Mags in my mind's eye. Her frame doting the same lavish leotard and tutu, hair secured high on her head.

"It's not her. It's not Mags," I kept telling myself. After an hour, I managed to fall back asleep. Only to have a nightmare.

"What do you mean you have cancer?" I cry out.

Charlotte's cheeks coat in wetness and her breathing erratic while sobs wrack her body. Her arms wrap around her waist as she slumps forward. Her frame is so frail and sad.

"That's what they told me. I don't remember much else. I didn't hear anything after. I just... stopped listening."

"What can they do? What can I do?" Every part of me is in hyper-drive. Every part of me wants to make this go away. To fix her. To help her get past this.

"I don't know. Mom knew I stopped paying attention to them. She told me it's at the point where no form of treatment will help. All we can do is just live my remaining time to the fullest."

This can't be happening! What the hell did she ever do to deserve this?! Not a damn thing! If anything, she is a saint walking the Earth. I just can't comprehend how this came to be. But watching her right now—as I hold her in my arms while her body shakes from her never-ending tears—I know I need to be her strength. I sure as hell don't like what is happening to her, but I must be strong for her. Fight with her, for her.

Isn't that what you do for the ones you love? Fight to the very end.

I lean down and whisper into her ear. "Then that's what we'll do."

I locate the nearest pen and scrap of paper and we make a list of all the places she has ever wanted to see, the things she has never done, and we set out to do as many as we can with the time gifted to us.

When I hand the list to Charlotte, an electric buzz zaps me. I glance at her face, confused by the current. Instead of seeing dark-blonde locks and green eyes, I'm met with Mags' chocolate waves and her glorious hazels.

I collapse on the floor, leaning onto the cool tiled wall. My stomach rolls again and I pinch my eyes tight. *Why am I dreaming of Charlotte? Who morphs into Mags?*

"Fuck!" The room spins and I grab the sides of the toilet. My body convulses and I dry heave into the porcelain. God, this fucking sucks.

A few minutes pass and I open my eyes. The room has stabilized and I crawl toward the sink. Hoisting myself up, I splash cold water over my face and neck. Bracing myself on the edges of the counter, I hang my head and regulate my breathing.

Losing Charlotte changed my view on life. Moments had more meanings. Memories were only pictures in your head that no one else could see, but that had more value than almost anything laid in your hands.

Losing her also made me see love different. I didn't want to love anyone after her. After having her ripped away, it felt wrong to fall in love again. After all, the universe was punishing us in some perverse manner. Perhaps we loved each other too much.

But isn't that the purpose of our existence?

To love and be loved. What else is there when love is gone?

After Charlotte, I shut down my heart. Built a towering fortress around it with the deepest of moats. Those who knew me said a part of me died with Charlotte. They were right. Charlotte owned part of my heart, and always would.

I vowed to never get in so deep again.

I vowed to never love again.

I vowed to never be susceptible to that type of loss again.

And once again... I failed.

And love has failed me.

Has my brain stirred up thoughts of Charlotte because of the messages I sent Mags?

I waited all night for a response, hopeful. She is busy, and I shouldn't have set an expectation in my mind. But God, I won't be able to breathe again until I hear from her. Until I see her again.

My phone pings from the bedroom and I all but run from the bathroom. Ripping it from the charging cord, I unlock the screen and see a text from Mags.

My breathing turns ragged. My heart in a vise. It's her. She's actually reaching out to me.

MAGDALENA

> I got your text. Things are busy, and HOT, here. I'll be here until Friday, to make sure she is comfortable. When I get back, I'll call and we can get together to talk. Sorry we fought before I left. I miss you.

I stare at the screen in shock. My head woozy for a different reason. My heart soaring. Her response unexpected since she is away working. But I'm elated she took the time to send something.

And she misses me.

We have a long way to go before things are anywhere near perfect again. But this is a start. A start I wasn't sure I would get. No matter what, I will do whatever it takes to earn her trust again. I will fix this.

CHAPTER 25

MAGDALENA

Nicole's uncle retrieves my suitcase from the trunk, extending the handle and wheeling it in my direction.

"I'll give you two a minute," he says, heading back to the car.

As soon as he steps away, Nicole wraps her arms around my waist. Her small frame wrings me harder than Lessa. Although I have only known her two-and-a-half weeks, Nicole holds a piece of my heart. A piece I plan to leave with her.

"You're so brave. And strong," I murmur against her hair. "I'm so proud of you."

She grips me tighter. "I don't want you to go, Mags."

"I wish I could stay, sweetie. But if you ever need me, I'm only a text or call away. I'll always listen."

She sniffles against my shirt. "You promise," she pleads.

"I promise," I assure her. "Now, go get in the car before your uncle gets in trouble for sitting there too long."

She nods and wipes her cheeks as she backs away. Just before she gets in the car, she spins around.

"Mags?"

"Yeah, sweetie?"

"Thank you." A lone tear rolls down her cheek before she hops in the car.

As the car drives away, my hand continues waving. "You're welcome," I whisper to myself.

I weave through the airport after checking my bag. After I get through TSA, I head for my gate and sit amongst the mass of travelers. There is another thirty minutes until they start boarding.

I'm eager to get back and sleep in my own bed again. Be in my own space again. And to see Geoff.

I grab my phone from my purse and unlock the screen. Seconds later, my finger hovers over the call symbol in Geoff's contact profile. My nerves quake, my fingers trembling.

I can do this.

I tap the call button and press the phone to my ear. It rings once. Twice. Three times.

Just as I'm tempted to end the call, Geoff's voice belts from the other end. He huffs, "Mags?"

"Yeah, it's me. Are you okay?"

His heavy breathing wanes. "I'm good. I was in Logan's office and didn't have my phone on me when it started ringing."

"Getting your cardio in for the day," I joke.

He's silent for a beat. "God, it's so good to hear your voice."

"Right back at ya," I confess. His voice is only one of many parts of him I miss. "Just wanted to let you know I'm boarding in a half hour. The flight's a little over six hours, so it'll be late when I get in."

"Do you need a ride home?" he offers.

"No, but thank you."

I'm sure he tried to disguise it, but I catch his muffled harrumph. I bite my lips to stop my laugh from escaping.

"After I check in at Statice in the morning, I'd like to come by and see you. Is noon good?"

"Will that give you enough time to get some sleep?" he asks. And I appreciate his concern.

"Yeah, I plan to stay awake on the plane. I'll be plenty tired when I get home."

"Okay, noon sounds great." The smile in his voice perceptible. "Have a safe flight. I'll see you tomorrow."

"See you tomorrow." *I miss you.*

The call disconnects before the words break free.

There is not enough caffeine in my bloodstream today. I drain the last of my chai tea latte, making far too much noise with the straw. The only time I resort to this coveted drink is when exhaustion strikes. Time zones are the enemy, I swear it.

"Hey, sweetheart," Beatrice says as she walks into my office. "What are you doing here?"

"I just wanted to jot a couple notes in Nicole's file before I forget. I'll only be here a little longer."

Beatrice scans over me, her eyes appraising. "You look drained. Go home. This stuff will be here on Monday."

I peek up from the computer. "It's just the time difference. I'm fine. And I'd rather do it now."

Beatrice sits in the chair across from me, leaning forward. "Don't give me that *I'm fine* nonsense. You're trying to do right by Nicole, I get it. But what about yourself?"

I stare at her a moment. These kids are important. "What about me? I may be busy, but I can't not help these kids."

"That's not what I'm saying," Beatrice coaxes.

"Well, then I'm confused."

"Sweetheart, I know you want to help these kids. And your dedication is wonderful. But you can't forget to live your own life. Be young. Fall in love. Start a family." She watches me with interest. "Don't become me. Someone who dedicated her life to helping others and goes home to an empty house. Be more than your career. Travel and see the world. I'd give anything to have someone waiting for me at home."

My heart swells and tears threaten to spill. Of all the conversations I've had with Beatrice, this was not one I would have predicted. Our mutual love to help these kids was another part of our bond. I didn't want to lose that.

"I don't know what else to do with my life," I confess, tears escaping and emotion clogging my throat.

"You don't need all the answers now, sweetheart. But you shouldn't spend every waking hour in this place. You'll only find a piece of happiness here. The rest is out in the world, waiting for you."

"But what if it's not? What if the happiness I thought I had isn't true? What if I messed up my one opportunity?"

Beatrice rises from her chair and walks around the desk, taking me in her arms. God, I love her hugs. Different than how I love Lessa's. Beatrice cocoons you like a newborn, warm and snug. Her faint bergamot scent resembling home. I never want this to end.

She releases me, framing my face in her hands. "I love you, Mags. It's time you start loving you too. And it's also time to start believing good things are meant for you."

WELCOME
to
LAKE LAVENDER

The drive to Geoff's house is a blur. But in the blink of an eye, I'm winding down his street and parking behind his navy BMW.

I cut the engine, but remain glued to my seat a minute. We have so much to talk about. My only hope is he'll be more forthcoming. About himself, Charlotte.

Most of all, I pray I can forgive him for what he did. His actions were deplorable. But doesn't everyone deserve a chance at forgiveness? An opportunity to fix their mistakes. I need that chance just as much as the next person.

You can do this.

I step out of my car and follow the small cobblestone path to his front door. No matter how many times I've walked from the driveway to his door, tonight feels different. Like coming home for the first time after a long journey. A journey we both needed to take.

The autumn air sweeps hair across my face. Hints of pine and fireplaces burning filter through the air. I inhale the comforting scents and beg they'll help settle my nerves.

After a second of hesitation, I rap my knuckles on the door before shoving them back in my coat pocket. Three breaths later, the door swings open.

I gasp when I take in Geoff's appearance. We have been apart two weeks, yet he looks like he's aged years. His face has lost some of its muscle and is sallow. His pants hang lower on his hips and his shirt swallows him a little. The Caribbean blues I love have lost some of their shimmer.

But his smile… I'm blinded by his happiness to see me.

"Hey," he says, a soft lilt in his voice. "Please, come inside."

I smile and step past him, scanning his living room. A fire crackles below the hearth, warming the space. Pine-scented cleaner perfumes the air. Everything tidy. Too tidy.

My fingers tremble in my pockets. My skin prickling with perspiration. And without a doubt, Geoff is studying every move I make. His stare is heavy on me. From removing my coat to my fumbling fingers to my inability to look him in the eyes, his questions weigh heavy in the air.

He steps up beside me and takes my coat. "Would you like anything? Water?"

I nod. "Water would be great. Thanks."

I sit on the couch, wiping my hands down my thighs. *Why am I so nervous?*

Geoff walks back from the kitchen, handing me the glass. I drink half the water. The cool water providing me with a hint of relief.

"I'm sorry," Geoff states as he sits beside me. "What I did was wrong. I have never been angrier with myself. And I'm sorry."

I set the glass on the table and turn to face him. "Thank you."

There were so many things I wanted to say to Geoff, but they all vanish. It isn't just about his apology. Something about being around him makes my brain forget how to operate. *I should have written it down.*

"When you walked out my door," Geoff starts. "I forgot how to breathe. And it was like my world crumbled away. For the second time."

He reaches for my hand and I let him take it. I crave his touch just as much as he does mine. As his fingers trace my hand, that warm familiar buzz returns. I love the jolt only he gives me. Like fireflies sparking to life inside me.

I close my eyes a moment. "I had to," I murmur.

He brings my hand between both of his. "I know you did. And I'm glad. Because if you hadn't, I don't think I would've gotten the reality check I needed."

"Oh?" I question, opening my eyes.

"Yes." He nods, inhaling a deep breath. "It needed to happen this way. So I could see what I lost, but also what I have a chance to gain again."

His fingers trace the lines of mine. *God, I missed his touch.*

"I should have done this in the beginning. Hopefully it's not too late," he confesses. "I'd like to tell you more. About Charlotte. And my family."

Mags' hazels widen with questions. "Only if you're ready," she says.

How can this woman be such a saint? After everything I did. After my despicable behavior. How can she grant me kindness?

Because that's who she is. Kind. Loving. Gentle.

I rub circles on her skin with my thumb, a tingle coursing through me at the contact. "I'm ready."

For a beat, I stare at our locked hands. *Inhale. Exhale.*

"Take your time." Her eyes soften when I look up.

We sit a moment. The occasional crackle from the fire the only sound. Her touch the only encouragement I need. *You've got this.*

"I first met Charlotte during my freshman year of high school. I caught sight of her in Algebra. Thirteen going on fourteen, girls weren't something I'd given much thought. Until her."

I pause. Within the last minute, she has pulled her legs up

and sits crisscrossed, facing me. Our hands still connected. Her eyes watching me intently. And I love how she focuses all her attention on me and what I'm telling her.

"Within a week, we were holding hands. After a month, we'd gone on a date—even though we had to ask our parents to drive us. She was my best friend, and I hers."

A tear rolls down my cheek and I ignore it, knowing more will follow.

"Her schedule was always full, but we managed to sneak in time together every day. Sometimes, after school and on the weekends, I'd watch her at the ballet studio where she practiced."

Mags jerks and sucks in a ragged breath. My eyes dart between hers, wondering what I'd said. But her expression remains stoic.

"Please continue," she croaks, her voice thick with emotion.

"Did I say something wrong?"

She shakes her head. "Until my mom died, I danced. It was unexpected is all. Please…"

What an odd coincidence. Both Charlotte and Mags had done ballet. It explains the paintings I'd seen in Mags' house but never asked about. I just assumed she appreciated the artistry. Strange. I shake off my distracted thoughts and continue.

"Between school, her dance practice, and studying, we didn't have much free time together. But when we did, we were never apart. The years passed and we grew closer than ever. Anyone who knew us, talked about us as if we were a unit."

I inhale deep and shift my gaze away from Mags, staring at a photo of me and the guys on a fishing trip a few years back. *You've got this.*

"It's okay," Mags whispers. She leans forward and presses her lips against my damp cheek.

A moment passes and I bring my eyes back into focus. *Inhale. Exhale.*

"As our senior year approached, Charlotte and I started talking about college and living together. She applied to a few dance schools, but her dream was to attend Juilliard. So, I applied to schools in New York. Everything looked so bright and shiny for us. Then, a couple weeks after my eighteenth birthday, Charlotte began complaining of abdominal pains. She played them off as not eating or drinking enough. After the pains persisted for more than a month, she finally told her mom."

Mags squeezed my hand tighter. She knew what was coming. I'd already explained Charlotte's diagnosis to her the night of the carnival. And I'm glad she held my hand right now. Like she was my lifeline. Because that's exactly what she was... my lifeline. The only person who could bring me back from the depths.

"After her diagnosis, we sat down with pen and paper. We wrote down everything we wanted to do together, in addition to things Charlotte thought she'd do alone. Like dance at Juilliard. The list was long, but we were determined to do as many as possible. We accomplished almost everything."

I take a moment to swipe the tears from my face, and Mags does the same. Her eyes are puffy and red and wet. The moment is sad, but I don't want to see her cry. I give us both another minute to collect ourselves and then continue.

"After Charlotte died, I lost myself. The thought of living without her was incomprehensible. My parents followed my every move. And if they couldn't, they asked someone else to. I was surrounded, but had never felt more alone. When their need to safeguard me never let up, I accepted a college offer far from home. I just needed an escape."

I hang my head and sigh. Mags slips her hands from mine and cradles my head, pressing a gentle kiss to the crown of my head.

"Where did you move from?" she whispers.

Of all the questions she could ask, she chooses this. If I were in her shoes, I would be asking more about Charlotte. Or my parents. Maybe she will, but doesn't want to start there. Maybe she wants to start from the beginning.

"Denver. I miss it there but don't think I could live there again. Not after everything." I lift my head and gauge her mood. A bit somber with a glint of curiosity.

"Have you been back since…" She trails off.

"Since Charlotte's death?"

She nods.

"No. I left near the end of summer that year and haven't gone back."

"What about your parents?"

"I call them from time to time. Probably not as often as I should. The first few years were difficult. All they ever asked was *how are you feeling* or said *I saw Charlotte's mom at the store.* It was still too raw. So the calls lessened. Now, I reach out on holidays or special occasions only."

Mags' face drops. "Do they ever come visit you?"

"No."

Her expression shifts and I wouldn't doubt she is trying to figure out how to mend me and my past.

"Geoff, can I say something and you not get offended?"

What is she thinking? I haven't the slightest idea. I'm a bit leery, yet curious. But I nod.

"Time is sacred. Don't waste it. Denver may be full of sad memories, but I'm sure there are tons of happy ones also. Don't rob yourself of happiness, Charlotte wouldn't want that for you. She wouldn't want you to lose your family because of her."

"I don't blame her," I retort.

"That may be true. Being in Denver is painful, I get it. But maybe it's time to try again."

Is it time? It has been a little more than ten years since I packed my bags and didn't look back. Was it time for me to go back? To visit my parents. Maybe stop by Charlotte's parents' house as well. A rock drops in the pit of my stomach, my hands shaking. I don't know if I can do this.

"You can do this," Mags says as if she can hear my thoughts. "I'll go with you, if you'd like."

I nod. "Only if you go with me. I'm not sure I'd have the strength to follow through without you."

Mags runs her fingers down the sides of my face, brushing the length of my hair back. She leans into me and presses her lips to mine. Warmth and hope and love pass from her lips to mine.

When our lips break apart, she holds my gaze. "I would be honored to go with you. And Geoff?"

"Hmm?"

"Thank you."

"For what?" I ask.

"For trusting me with a piece of you."

She doesn't just have a piece of me, she has all of me. And I couldn't imagine a single day without her. So when I open my mouth to speak, there is no hesitation. Not an ounce of doubt. She is my forever and I belong to her.

"I love you," I tell her clear as day.

Her cheeks flush, eyes bouncing between mine. A single tear rolls down her cheek. "I love you, too."

CHAPTER 27
MAGDALENA

Three months later

The deep resonance of Geoff's laugh trumps the conversation in the living room. Everyone's voice is muffled, but it's clear they're talking about something. I'm curious what is so funny.

When I peek my head around the doorway of the kitchen, he's on the couch, Logan's phone circulating around the room. Just as I'm about to ask, the craziest snort-laugh leaves Lessa's body. I don't think I've ever heard her do that before. Whatever they're looking at, it must be hysterical.

"What am I missing out on here?" I ask with my hands held up, coated in beer batter from the onions I was just dredging.

"You have to see this!" Lessa waves me toward her.

"Seriously guys, it's not that funny. Can we please just stop with the show and tell." Owen's words are more of a request

"Dude, memories. What can I say? They have a special place in my heart," Logan says, a laugh rolling off his tongue as he presses his hand to his heart. The look they exchange is awkward—Logan amused, Owen not so much.

"I can't recall any time where you wanted to walk down memory lane, except when it's to laugh at me. Seriously Logan, must I always be the brunt of the joke?"

"Dude, you just make it too easy."

Walking through the living room, I keep my hands angled so I don't drip batter everywhere. My eyes land on the ballerina paintings for a split-second and I smile. After Geoff and I flew to Denver two months ago, I offered to take the paintings down.

Visiting his parents, and Charlotte's, was hard on him. But that was nothing compared to our visit of Charlotte's cemetery plot. The moment we approached the beautifully decorated Aspen white marble, tears flooded us both. Geoff cried for the woman he lost so young. I cried for the woman who missed out on too much of her life.

It was an emotional trip for us both. So, when we returned and I walked past the paintings, I offered to replace them with something new. Geoff said no. It reminds us both where we came from and what we have overcome to be where we are today.

I reach Lessa's side and look at the photo on Logan's phone screen. It must've been taken while they were in college, their features a little more baby-faced than they now seem. Geoff is on the right, tongue out and his right hand signaling the person behind the camera to *rock on*. Logan is on the left, his lips puckered and about to graze Owen's left cheek. Owen is in the middle, passed out, and plastered with eyeshadow, liner, blush, and lipstick. And somehow, they've even managed to get a dress on him.

My hand flies to my mouth, attempting to subdue my laughter, coating my face with batter. If I would've gone to college, surely Lessa, Lena, and I would have been doing pranks like this too. Somehow, I'll have to make up for those lost opportunities, which could easily happen with my present company. "Oh my god, that's hysterical!"

A phone camera snaps and captures an image of my face smeared with batter.

"That one's going in the vault." Owen's grin spreads from ear to ear.

Before I get a word out, the chime of five different phones fills the room. And now all of us have a picture of my batter face. *Great.* This one will live on for years to come.

"Awe, babe, I think it's adorable," Geoff says. "I think I'll make it the background on my phone."

"Whatever." My half-smile and wink the last thing he sees before I head back to the kitchen.

As I finish making the last of the finger foods, conversation fills the air, the guys trying to explain their passion for architecture to the ladies, whose interests are far from that of structural designs. But as I add the last of the food to empty platters, the living room goes quiet. Oddly quiet. As if they're conspiring. *What are they up to out there?*

My bare feet thump across the floor. In the living room, every single one of them is engaged in something different—magazine, cell phone, newspaper, fiddling with the remote, straightening pillows. *Weird.*

"Food's ready, whoever wants to eat," I announce.

As if a school fire drill has sounded, they all jump up from their seats and pile into the kitchen.

Yep, something is definitely going on.

Plate in hand, Geoff comes up beside me, resting his hand on my lower back and his lips atop my head. "Everything looks great, babe. I'm so glad we decided to have these get-togethers. Having our family together once a week, I can see its appeal."

"Me too. It's the best form of therapy, being surrounded by people we love."

We all meander into the living room, situating ourselves with mountains of high-calorie foods. One of our new traditions —the six of us all together on Saturday evenings. Didn't matter where we were. Didn't matter what we did. As long as we were together, it was perfect. It was one of the best decisions.

"So, did anyone decide on a game while I was cooking?"

Lena begins speaking, food packed in her cheeks. I laugh, half tempted to tell her she looks like a chipmunk. But I resist.

"The guys suggested Monopoly. But Lessa and I vetoed it," Lena says.

"Okay. Well, we have plenty of options. Shouldn't be too hard to pick one," I suggest. We all go quiet, munching on our food. And the silence reminds me... "Why were you guys being so quiet after I went back into the kitchen?"

Every set of eyes darts around the room for a second before landing on Geoff. Interesting. Is he up to something?

"What?" he asks before stuffing his mouth with a mini corn dog.

Lessa and Lena roll their eyes at him. Owen and Logan shovel food into their mouths like they've never eaten. Or been taught proper manners. They're an interesting duo.

Whatever. I'll get whatever he is avoiding out of him. It is only a matter of time.

After another minute of no talking and food crunching, I

grab a handful of games for us to pick from. A few debates later, and Geoff is shuffling a deck of cards for Texas Hold'em. We don't play for money, just bragging rights. I have yet to win those rights.

Five hands later, I am staring at my first real chance at winning. I have won three of the four hands, Owen winning the other. If I can pull off this one and one more, victory is mine.

Everyone around the table has put on their best poker face —something I have difficulty maintaining. The room is quiet and serious. You'd think we were in a casino and the winner would walk away with millions.

All bets and cards have been set. Starting with Lena, everyone shows their cards. As each one flips, I grow more and more excited. I flash my cards, throwing my hands up in victory. "Yes! Read 'em and weep."

Geoff clears his throat beside me. "Sorry, babe." His frown is adorable, but it soon morphs into a smile.

Dammit.

"I had a really good hand," I whine.

"Yes, you did. Unfortunately for you, mine was better."

"Maybe next game night." I sulk as Geoff kisses my forehead.

With the game wrapped up, we all start cleaning up. We have hung out at my house enough on Saturdays, everyone has their own cleanup jobs. After Geoff and I finish the dishes, we join everyone in the living room.

Idle chitchat continues for a couple minutes before Lessa breaks up all conversation. "So, Mags…"

"So, Lessa…" I mock.

"How long have you guys been together now?"

That came out of left field. I study her face a moment, curious. *What is she up to?*

"Nine months next week. Why?" I drawl.

"That's more than enough time," she states, not really talking to me.

"More than enough time for what?" *What the hell is she talking about?* Sometimes, she is just weird.

"Nothing," she singsongs, going back to her phone as if the conversation never existed.

I glance around the room, thoroughly confused. Everyone except Geoff is glued to their cell phone. A moment later, Owen and Logan rise from their seats. They give each other a pointed look before glancing over at Lessa and Lena—who are now on their feet. Everyone starts heading for the door, yet none of them have said a word.

What the hell is going on?

"Everything okay?" I ask, directing my question at anyone who will answer.

"Yeah, I'm just really beat," Owen answers. "It's been a long week."

Okay. I will accept his answer, but what does that have to do with the other three. And the rest of their eyes dart away from mine like they're trying to hide something.

I am so confused.

"I rode over with Owen, so I'm kind of obligated to go when he's ready," Logan states.

"And I came over with Lessa," Lena chimes in. "She told me we'd have to leave early because of something to do with inventory at the café." She shrugs. "I just figured we'd leave now since the guys were."

Their excuses are a bit too perfect, but I let them slide. This time.

"Okay. Well, let me walk you out."

We all shuffle to the door where hugs and goodbyes are exchanged. Within a few minutes, Geoff and I are alone. We clean up and put everything back in its place. And a moment later, we're sitting on the couch with our hands woven together.

Geoff shifts beside me before he leans into me, his body heating mine. I breathe in his sweet teakwood and musk scent and close my eyes as it relaxes me. There is no better place than Geoff's side.

In the last nine months, we have been through so much together. Digging deep inside ourselves. Awakening old wounds and healing them together. If it weren't for Geoff, I don't know if I'd be where I am now. Truly living my life, surrounded by the most amazing friends, and next to the man I love.

Geoff kisses my cheek before leaning his against mine. "I have a question," he whispers.

He is so close. But never close enough.

"Mmmhm."

"Do you want to move in together?"

I lean back and look into the crystalline blues I love. He is one-hundred percent serious. Have we reached this stage of our relationship? *Cohabitating?* There isn't a diagram to tell you when it's right. You just know.

Do I want to live with Geoff? Yes. We're practically living together already.

Is it time? I don't know. Yes? I think.

Just be yourself.

The love residing in those words is all the encouragement I need.

My hazels get lost in the depths of Geoff's blues. We may

have had a rocky moment or two, but you can't deny your heart what it wants. And from the moment I met Geoff, he was all my heart wanted. All my heart will ever need.

"Yes. I would love nothing more."

EPILOGUE

MAGDALENA

Two Years Later

"That's all our time today, Jan. Remember to use the tools we talked about if you start feeling claustrophobic again."

I rise from the chair behind my desk and walk with my client to the door. She hesitates a moment but stands from the couch. We walk to the door as Jan's fingers fidget in front of her.

"I will, Dr. Bishop." No matter how many times I hear that title, it still sounds bizarre. "Have a good weekend."

"You too."

I close out my notes for the day and save my files before shutting down my computer. It is still so surreal to have my own practice. Just me. Maybe one day, I'll add another doctor to the practice. But everything is still fresh and new.

A couple weeks after Geoff and I visited Denver two years ago, I mentioned how I wanted to do more to help people. Not only children but adults as well. After everything we had experienced in our past—and not dealt with—I wanted to help others like us. It just felt like it was my calling.

When we returned to Lake Lavender, Geoff encouraged me to go back to school and finish my Doctor of Psychology degree. I hesitated at first but followed through. By doubling my course load, I was able to complete my degree in less than two years.

And as of last month, I had an incredible new degree on my office wall. It rested beneath glass and was surrounded by a beautiful wooden frame Lessa and Lena gave me as a congratulations.

Architectural Crimson helped build my office, after I told the guys my ideas. One year into school and the office was almost finished. It was unreal to watch my ideas come to life. Seeing my ideas transform into pictures and designs was fascinating. I loved the entire process.

The only thing *off* was not seeing Beatrice every day. I missed her. A lot.

A few months into my studies, I was having trouble balancing time for school and Statice. Beatrice caught on quick and suggested I cut back my time at the center. We debated the topic for weeks before I gave in. I had been so exhausted.

The first month, I reduced my time by half. The second month, I cut it in half again. By the time the third month rolled around, Beatrice told me to focus on my studies. Guilt rattled me for days. Leaving Statice felt like betrayal. Leaving those kids had me antsy and uncomfortable.

But Beatrice assured me the kids were doing well, and everyone was cheering me on. And their support meant the world to me.

A year-and-a-half later and I am the proud owner of Lavandula Health, and the only psychologist office—besides Statice

—in town that caters to teens and adults under twenty-five. It is a major accomplishment, and I'm lucky to have had so many people encouraging me.

I pack my laptop in my bag and sling it over my shoulder alongside my purse. I lock up then hop in my car, send Geoff a quick message to let him know I'm on my way, and drive off.

Main Street is already bustling, and it's only five o'clock. Geoff and I will be in the Main Street crowd with the group tomorrow night for our weekly hangout. It's the best tradition we ever started.

Geoff's car is parked in the driveway when I get home and I pull up beside him. When we agreed to move in together, we hadn't really thought of the logistics. After nights of discussion, we decided he move into my house. It had more space and held years of good memories. His house had only been a place he slept in.

I unlock the front door and step into the foyer, setting my bag and purse on the table.

"Hello," I call into the dim house.

No answer.

When I step farther into the living room, candle flickers catch my eyes. I step closer and vanilla wafts the air around me. A twine-wrapped bundle of red roses lays beside it with a note.

"Someone's being romantic," I say into the darkened room.

From the back of the house, light laughter floats in the air. But he doesn't come out to greet me. *What's he up to?*

I pick up the note and read it as quiet music starts playing from the soundbar. "XO" by John Mayer. The song makes me smile.

Mags, please forgive me in advance for my somewhat public display

tonight. I'm not the most creative person on the planet, but this was
a moment I wanted to share with you and the people most important
to us. Follow the rose petals.

Before I follow the petals to wherever they lead, I reach for the roses and bring them to my nose. I inhale deep and revel in the fragrance. A moment later, I stuff the note in my pocket and follow the trail of flower petals scattered along the floor.

When I reach the dining room table, there is another candle and note. Alongside it is a photo. I pick it up and realize it is one of me, one I didn't realize he had snapped. I am standing in the center of the dance floor, Lessa and Lena off to my side, in the nightclub of Black Silk. My face plastered with a brief smile, disguising my lack of comfort.

But the way he has captured the image, it changes the way I see myself. At this moment, I was beautiful. I'd never seen myself like this; from his perspective. And the way he saw me was incredible.

I read the note perched against the candle.

From the moment I saw you, I had to know you.
Had to meet you. Even if just to say hello.

You lured me in. Pulled me like a magnet.
The sound of your sweet voice. The gift of your name.

The first song fades and the piano intro of "Latch" by Sam Smith floats in the air. I tuck the photo and note in my pocket and follow the petals to the spare bedroom.

Inside is a third note and a new photo. In the new photo, I am standing outside of Statice, the breeze blowing my hair off to the side. My hands fumbling for my sunglasses.

I remember this day. When Geoff first found me after the club. His forward nature making me a little uncomfortable.

I couldn't sleep that night, after seeing you in Black Silk.
All I could think about was 'I need to find this woman'.

I went back to Black Silk, telling them a tale to see if
they'd give me more info. A dead end.

Then, fortune was on my side. I went for coffee and bumped
into your best friend. Call it fate. Destiny.
Whatever you'd like. In that moment, I knew it was meant to be.

So, I drove to your work. Waiting for you to leave.
I know. Creepy. But I wouldn't change anything.
You agreed to go on a date.

I laugh, remembering how freaked out I was that he pursued me. Stuffing the new mementos in my pocket, I hurry to the next candle and note. The trail leads me to the office. When I reach the next photo, it steals my breath.

I hadn't known he'd taken any of these pictures so far. If I'd known in the beginning, I would have probably thought he was a creep. But now… I love every single one. Each portraying different moments in our relationship and how he felt about each moment.

Are the pictures intimate? *Definitely*.

Am I bothered that my friends might have seen them? *Maybe a little*.

The current photo is the most intimate yet. A photo of the two of us. Me asleep, my head resting on his shoulder, his arm around me, my arm across his chest. My breasts hidden by my arm, his eyes closed and cheek pressed to my hair. In this photo… Geoff is on cloud nine. Not just regarding sexual satisfaction, but more in the sense of life fulfillment.

Ellie Goulding's "How Long Will I Love You" floats through the air now. And I pick up the newest note.

In this single moment, our first night together, I knew I loved you.
And that thought… It was euphoric and frightening.
We barely knew each other, but I knew.

From that moment on, all I could think about was you.
How much time I could spend with you. The things we could
do together. The things we could learn about one another.

I wanted to know everything there was to know about you.
What made you happy. What made you sad. If I made you happy.
If you wanted me as much as I wanted you.

My eyes well, the tears struggling to not fall, my vision blurring. *Where is he?* I'm not sure how much of this I can handle. My heart is going to explode from this trip down memory lane. Never has my soul felt so complete… whole.

Securing the photo and note with the others, I dash out of the room and head for our bedroom. The trail ends at our bed, where one last candle and note rests.

One last song…
When it starts, walk onto the porch.

The strumming sounds of a guitar rolls out of the speaker, and I try to place the song. The lyrics begin and I step onto the porch off of our bedroom. Geoff stands beside a three-wick candle. He's in a navy button-down and jeans.

Why is he wearing that? Shouldn't he still be in his suit from work?

I listen to the words of the song, realization striking. He reaches forward and takes my hand in his before he lowers onto one knee.

My heart starts running a marathon in my chest, the light sheen on his palm suddenly noticeable.

His left hand digs in the pocket of his denim and retrieves a small box.

Waterfalls cascade down my cheeks, the words from "Marry Me" by Train setting the scene.

Geoff glances at his left palm, his fingers clenched tightly together. He meets my eyes again, his nervousness evident in the lines of his smile. He inhales deep, his blues never straying from my hazel.

"Magdalena Violet Bishop, it's not always easy to put my feelings for you into words. From the first moment I saw you on the dance floor in the club, I knew you were more than a beautiful woman, garnering my attention. There was this unseen, unspoken force, bringing us together. The universe telling us we were supposed to meet, to be something more than two people passing by one another. Although we both had histories restraining our hearts, we effortlessly grew closer, love building stronger by the hour. Our lives interconnecting."

He pauses a second, glancing over his shoulder. I follow where he looked, but see nothing.

"We've had our ups, we've had our downs, and we've shared our darkest secrets along with the most joyous. Over the last three years, almost, we've built so many memories.

Memories that will stick with me forever. And now... now I want to create a whole new set of memories.

"Magdalena, I love you. I love you beyond comprehension. If I could extract the feeling from my chest and put it in yours, just so you could feel it, just once, I would. I never imagined such a passion existed until I met you. I cannot envision my life without you, nor do I wish to. Dr. Magdalena Violet Bishop, will you marry me? Will you spend the rest of eternity with me?"

The waterworks gush from my tear ducts and won't quit, tears of happiness in endless supply. Geoff reaches in his other pocket and pulls out a tissue and hands it to me.

Working hard to locate my voice, I clear my throat and prepare to deliver the words that will change our lives forever.

Something moves in my periphery and I glance past Geoff's shoulder once more. And that's when I notice the back yard is lit in twinkling lights and our friends fill the space. Along with Geoff's parents and Beatrice.

They all knew? And no one said a word.

"Geoffrey Marcus Lawson, that was more than incredible. I know love cannot be translated into any language, but you translate it better than anyone I've ever known. You've shown me so much more than love and how to love again. I never want to imagine a day without you or the love we share. *Yes!* I will marry you."

As soon as I say the words, Geoff slides a platinum band with a sparkling square-cut diamond on my finger. He stands and cups my face. "I love you so much, Mags."

"I love you, too."

Cheers and congratulations can be heard for miles. Geoff draws me close and cocoons me in his arms. Everyone else fades to the background because this is all that matters. Him. Us. Together.

"I love you. Forever and ever," I whisper into his chest.

He kisses the top of my head before meeting my eyes. "I love you. Always."

And then he drops his lips to mine and I get lost in his kiss.

ONE NIGHT FORSAKEN
LAKE LAVENDER SERIES—BOOK TWO

One night. No names. No romance. Just fun. Nothing more—at least, that's what she tells herself. Until he appears in her coffee shop months later with that addictive smile. She swore off commitment. He vows to never love again. But the more they fight it, the more life brings them together.

ONE NIGHT FORSAKEN TROPES
🌙 One night stand
😳 Acquaintances to friends with benefits
🌲 Small town Washington
🚫 Commitment phobes
👀 Cinnamon roll hero
☕ Quirky coffee shop owned by heroine

Get ready for One Night Forsaken, book two in the Lake Lavender Series.

A NOTE ON DEPTHS AWAKENED

When I first wrote Depths Awakened, it was intended to be a standalone romance. As my debut novel, I didn't want to overwhelm myself with creating a series when I was new to authorship and publishing.

Years later, stories centering around Mags's friends popped in my head. I considered updating Depths Awakened to my current writing style and adding more to the characters and town, but decided to leave it as is (I like to see the progress I've made) and focus energy on the next story.

With One Night Forsaken and Every Thought Taken, you will see Mags and Geoff again, plus different glimpses of the town. I loved coming back to Lake Lavender, seeing the small town with fresh eyes, and writing new stories you will love. Depths Awakened may not flow as seamlessly with One Night Forsaken and Every Thought Taken, but I tried to make them as cohesive as possible.

MORE BY PERSEPHONE

The Click Duet

High school sweethearts torn apart. When fate gives them a second chance, one doesn't trust they won't be hurt again. Through the Lens (Click Duet #1) and Time Exposure (Click Duet #2) is an angsty, second chance, friends to lovers romance with all the feels.

The Inked Duet

A man with a broken heart and a woman scared to put herself out there. Love is never easy. Sometimes love rips you apart. Fine Line (Inked Duet #1) and Love Buzz (Inked Duet #2) is a second chance at love, single parent romance with a pinch of angst and dash of suspense.

The Artist Duet

A tortured hero with the biggest heart and a charismatic heroine with the patience of a saint. Previous heartache has him fighting his desire to be more than friends with her. But she is everywhere, and he can't help but give in. The Artist Duet is an angsty, friends to lovers slow burn.

Transcendental

A musician in search of his muse and a woman grieving the loss of her husband. Two weeks at an exclusive retreat and their connection rivals all others. Until she leaves early without notice. But he refuses to give up until he finds her again.

Broken Sky

Their eyes meet across the bar, but she looks away first. Does her best to give him zero attention. But when he crowds her on the dancefloor, she can't deny the instant chemistry. After one night together, he marks her as his. Unfortunately, another woman thinks he belongs to her.

Distorted Devotion

Swept off her feet by love, life takes a dark, unexpected turn. Now the love of her life may be the cause of her death. Check out this gripping, romantic suspense.

Ink Veins

Persephone Autumn's debut poetry collection, Ink Veins, explores topics of depression, love, and self-discovery with a raw, unfiltered voice.

Broken Metronome

When the music of the heart dies...

Broken Metronome is an angsty poetry collection full of heartache and the possibility of what may have been.

THANK YOU

Thank you so much for reading **Depths Awakened**, book one in the Lake Lavender Series. If you would take a moment to leave a review on the retailer site where you made your purchase, Goodreads and/or BookBub, it would mean the world to me.

Reviews help other readers find and enjoy the book as well.

Much love,
   Persephone

DEPTHS AWAKENED PLAYLIST

Here are some of the songs from the *Depths Awakened* playlist. You can listen to the entire playlist on Spotify!

First Breath After Coma | Explosions In The Sky
Georgia | Vance Joy
Ocean Eyes | Billie Eilish
Dangerous Night | Thirty Seconds To Mars
Fantasy | Black Atlass
Apology Drawn/Gramercy Park | David Torn
Litost | X Ambassadors
Dust to Dust | The Civil Wars
U and I | blckbrn
I Found | Amber Run
All I Want | Kodaline
The Night We Met | Lord Huron feat. Phoebe Bridgers
Poison & Wine | The Civil Wars
You Are The Reason | Calum Scott & Leona Lewis

CONNECT WITH PERSEPHONE

Connect with Persephone
www.persephoneautumn.com

Subscribe to Persephone's newsletter
www.persephoneautumn.com/newsletter

Join Persephone's reader's group
Persephone's Playground

Follow Persephone online

instagram.com/persephoneautumn

facebook.com/persephoneautumnwrites

tiktok.com/@persephoneautumn

goodreads.com/persephoneautumn

bookbub.com/authors/persephone-autumn

amazon.com/author/persephoneautumn

pinterest.com/persephoneautumn

ACKNOWLEDGMENTS

Many thanks to my wife, for being patient while I trudged through this journey and poured hours upon hours into my writing, aside from my normal working hours. For months, I had zero down time. You have the patience of a saint when it comes to me. I love you!

Thank you to all of the authors in the Inkers Group, especially Alessandra Torre. Thank you for your knowledge and expertise, and for sharing your wisdom with the journey to pressing publish. Thank you for giving me that extra bit of courage and confidence. Your advice is invaluable.

Thank you, Gem. For scanning through my manuscript and being amazing at what you do and helping me feel a little less anxious about my first book baby!

Thank you Elizabeth of Razor Sharp Editing. For your expertise, advice, and knowledge. For your straight forward critique and suggestions. They are exactly what I needed. My first book baby wouldn't be where it is today without you.

Thank you Ellie of My Brother's Editor for putting the final polishes on Depths Awakened and deleting/adding punctuation. You're a rockstar!

Thank you to Abi at Pink Elephant Designs for the original cover and this stunning updated cover! Your covers are nothing short of perfection and I love this one more each time I look at it.

Thank you to all my friends and family who have supported my writing over the years. Pouring your head and heart onto pages for everyone to read is not always the easiest process. All of your kind words and praise makes this journey that much sweeter.

Thank you to everyone who purchases this book and reads it. This book has been slowly coming to life over the last four to five years. Thank you for choosing to read my words. You have no idea how appreciative I am.

ABOUT THE AUTHOR

USA Today Bestselling Author Persephone Autumn lives in Florida with her wife, crazy dog, and two lover-boy cats. A proud mom with a cuckoo grandpup. An ethnic food enthusiast who has fun discovering ways to vegan-ize her favorite non-vegan foods. If given the opportunity, she would intentionally get lost in nature.

For years, Persephone did some form of writing; mostly journaling or poetry. After pairing her poetry with images and posting them online, she began the journey of writing her first novel.

She mainly writes romance and poetry, but on occasion dips her toes in other works. Look for her non-romance publications under P. Autumn.

CPSIA information can be obtained
at www.ICGtesting.com
Printed in the USA
BVHW030856220123
656725BV00022B/695

9 781951 477622